Praise for *Ariel Crashes a Train*

★ "A revelatory, razor-sharp, and powerfully honest depiction of the reality of living with OCD."

—*Kirkus Reviews,* **starred review**

★ "Cole sharply exposes the legal shortcomings and binary fallacies that sometimes complicate healing. Vivid, emotionally charged verse renders terse, illuminating discussions of gender, race, religion, and sex that candidly contextualize OCD, and give teeth to this dazzling, layered story of self-acceptance and agency."

—*Publishers Weekly,* **starred review**

"*Ariel Crashes a Train* is a poetic, visceral, deeply affecting story that will stay with me for years to come, not only because of its beauty and intensity but because it's the first time I've seen OCD represented so accurately in fiction."

—**ALLISON BRITZ, author of** *Obsessed: A Memoir of My Life with OCD*

"A gorgeously kind, wonderfully gentle, and unfailingly compassionate depiction of obsessive-compulsive disorder. *Ariel Crashes a Train* and all its characters are bursting with light."

—**ASHLEY WOODFOLK, critically acclaimed author**
of *Nothing Burns as Bright as You*

Praise for *Dear Medusa*

★ "Both vulnerable and fierce, Cole boldly examines agency, bodily autonomy, and internalized misogyny."

—*Publishers Weekly*, starred review

★ "Cole's prose is beautiful, thought-provoking, and filled with emotion. . . . **This novel is one that readers won't put down willingly.**"

—*SLJ*, starred review

"Dazzling with clarity, blistering with anger. . . . This book is as wide in scope as it is economical in its language. **Illuminating.**"

—*Kirkus Reviews*

"Cole's novel in verse is a raw and uncompromising view into the sexualization of young women. She peels back the layers of Alicia's trauma, **fully immersing us in a world where we are cradled in Alicia's pain and then her subtle pinpricks of joy.**"

—*Booklist*

"This is more than a story about sexual violence— **this book is about race, sexuality, love, and how anger can be a catalyst for healing.**"

—GABRIELLE UNION, bestselling author, actress, and producer

ALSO BY OLIVIA A. COLE

Dear Medusa

ARIEL CRASHES A TRAIN

OLIVIA A. COLE

LR LABYRINTH ROAD | NEW YORK

Text copyright © 2024 by Olivia A. Cole
Jacket art copyright © 2024 by Beatriz Ramo

Visit us on the Web! GetUnderlined.com

Educators and librarians, for a variety of teaching tools,
visit us at RHTeachersLibrarians.com

Library of Congress Cataloging-in-Publication Data
Name: Cole, Olivia A., author.
Title: Ariel crashes a train / Olivia A. Cole.
Description: First edition. | New York: Labyrinth Road, 2024. | Audience: Ages 14+ | Audience: Grades 10–12. | Summary: Ariel grapples with her fear of her own mind and violent fantasies, driven by her desire to meet her parents' expectations and societal norms, until a summer job at a carnival leads her to new friends who help her discover her struggle with obsessive-compulsive disorder and find acceptance and support for her true self.
Identifiers: LCCN 2023031454 | ISBN 978-0-593-64466-9 (trade) | ISBN 978-0-593-64468-3 (ebook)
Subjects: CYAC: Novels in verse. | Friendship—Fiction. | Obsessive-compulsive disorder—Fiction. | Identity—Fiction. | LGBTQ+ people—Fiction | LCGFT: Novels in verse. | Novels.
Classification: LCC PZ7.5.C65 Ar 2024 | DDC [Fic]—dc23

The text of this book is set in 10.75-point Adobe Garamond Pro.

Editors: Liesa Abrams and Emily Shapiro
Cover Designer: Casey Moses
Interior Designer: Megan Shortt
Copy Editor: Barbara Bakowski
Managing Editor: Rebecca Vitkus
Production Manager: Natalia Dextre

Printed in the United States of America
10 9 8 7 6 5 4 3 2 1
First Edition

FOR OMAUN

I HAVE TO.

Every time I leave the kitchen
whether I'm going
in or out of the house.

It's a rule written in blood.

This morning, like every morning,
I stare down at the collection of kitchen knives
in the drawer by the stove.

There are ten of them, one for each finger,
short and long, serrated and not,

    silver silver silver

I know them all well.

    This is the rule: **in order to stop myself
    from driving one of them into my father's chest**

I must open the drawers—the silent kind
that don't slam—and tap each blade
with one finger, six times
for each knife:

tap
tap
tap
tap
tap
tap

I have to concentrate.
Each tap measured, firm.
On the third knife, the fifth tap is too soft.

I start over.

Two more times
until I get it right
and all the scales growing inside me
soften back into flesh
and smooth wet organs.

Only then can I go
to the front door.

Everyone is safe.
For now.

I'M GOING TO TRY ONE MORE TIME.

The bus stop is where I used to think my best thoughts—
maybe because there, the world
is as noisy as the inside of my head:

clangor and clamor and squeaking brakes
people nodding to music
and each other,
coming and going.

I can wear headphones with no music
and no one knows any different—
if my head twitches or my neck bends
they all think *MUSIC. That girl is into her music.*

On the bus, I can make myself small

all 5'11" of me balled
against the smudged window.

I am part of the scenery—we all are.

I haven't tried in one week
because it already happened once
and I wanted to give it time,
maybe let it fade.

Today it's not rush hour.
Today the rush is less rushing—

an old woman and her shopping bag
two young guys with backpacks

    and me.

A bus is coming but it's not ours
and the old woman has old woman eyes
so she can't see that it's the 44
not the 14
so she's stepping forward to the curb
expectantly
and the bus isn't slowing down

and then it happens.

I'm pushing her.
My muscles seize—
something green and scaly
nestled between ropes of my intestine
coming awake and thrashing its tail.

screech of the bus
sickening thud of steel
against eighty-year-old bones

shopping bag catches the wind
sweeps out into the street
a single apple rolls toward the sewer

and at first I'm running away
then, when my lungs shout,
walking. Four blocks away
I finally look back.

The 14 is pulling up and one of the guys
with backpacks holds the woman's shopping bag
while she climbs slowly on board.
The insistent beeping of the bus's
kneel ricochets down the block.

When the bus catches up to me,
the wind from it blowing by
throws my hair in a cyclone.

Three miles to go.

Other buses will come
but they're not an option anymore.

In the pit of my stomach
the crocodile is awake
and by now I know
that the only way to keep
        everyone safe
is by making sure the beast
has lots of space.

MEETING LEAH SHOULD FEEL LIKE COMFORT—
a friendship sprouted
on a school bus in fourth grade, both of us
small (even me, then) with big voices, yelling
at a boy who emptied his pencil sharpener
down the back of a girl's shirt.

Neither of us was afraid to use
the word *fuck* and when neither of us
got in trouble, it felt
like we were charmed,
that we had charmed each other.

Leah's voice has grown and grown:
president of the Jewish Student Union,
co-chair of the Young Chemists Society.

I asked her on Halloween if she'd outgrown me.

You can't outgrow what you're made for,
she'd said, but it didn't feel like an answer,
and lately it feels like even if she's not
outgrowing me,

then maybe the tree of her
is merely growing in another direction,
like the peace lily in my mom's office
always arching toward the window.

Leah has a boyfriend—Cesar—
with a smile like that: like the sun.
I don't blame her for leaning into him
when lately everything about me
is mist.

It's June but Leah wants hot chocolate
and these are the things I love about her,
but when I sink down across from her
I almost forget to smile.

Across the street, a cat stares at itself in a store window,
lashing its tail, suspicious of its own reflection.

I feel the same way
and this is why:

I DON'T DO IT ON PURPOSE.

But while Leah is stirring her cocoa, the steam
rising and curling like exhaust, her mouth
moving in the shapes of words, I am imagining

standing up from the table
and lifting its edge, sending
the hot brown liquid splashing
across Leah's bare chest
Leah screaming
Leah trying to get it off
Leah going to the hospital
for third-degree burns
me sitting and doing nothing

How hot is hot chocolate?
Hot enough to burn?
How hot does it have to be
to cause third-degree burns?
Is there a law for how hot coffee can be?
Would I be allowed to help or would she never
speak to me again?

Are you listening?

My hands are knotted under the table,
and my eyes had followed.

When they rise, there's Leah's face
frowning, but I'm still thinking
about her screaming, how she would sound
with her skin turning red then purple.

I don't do it on purpose.

I'm picturing blisters
    while she's asking me if I heard her
I'm wondering
if there's a first aid kit
in the coffee shop
    while she's asking me what my problem is

I tell her *I'm fine*
sorry
I got distracted.

IT'S LIKE MY BRAIN IS A STAGE MAGICIAN'S HAT

and somewhere inside me a wand is tapped on the rim
and suddenly a white rabbit appears from the dark mouth of
the hat
    except the rabbit is covered in blood
and it runs in circles around me onstage
and then from the hat leaps a fox and its teeth are dripping red
and I stare stare stare, wondering what it will sound like

the exact moment that the fox's teeth
sink into the rabbit's soft throat
and I can't avert my eyes.

All of this happening all the time, unable to look away,
my brain both fox and rabbit and also the hat
and
        especially
the teeth.

"WHAT ARE YOU THINKING ABOUT?"

"Nothing."
What else can I say?

This isn't
Be careful, you might spill that.

This is
Oh, I was just thinking about what would happen
if I flipped the table and boiling liquid burned your skin
and whether I would help you or just watch.

In the last year I have watched
Leah get farther and farther away
as I drift deeper down
what feels like a tunnel
flickering in fluorescent light.

I imagine telling her the truth,
watching her eyes widen
then shrink
then all of her pulling fully
out of reach.

I would rather keep my secrets
and
keep her close.

HOW DO I EXPLAIN

the wrongness
    that sits in the core of me like the rotten pit of a
    soft-bodied fruit
the wrongness
    that feels like the seed from which everything grows?

How do I look when no one is watching? I study
photographs, wondering if the face I see is my real face

or if there are moments when it morphs,
where the hidden crocodile is visible and vulgar.

What if someone takes a photo of that?
Caught on camera, my whole life red-handed.

LEAH KNOWS ALL MY OTHER SECRETS

even the ones I don't write poems about:

getting my first period in gymnastics, leaving blood
on the beam—Coach walking around checking
everyone for cuts, Leah laughing so hard she peed,
both of us washing
leotards in her basement that night.

Me pretending to like Pentatonix
for my entire seventh grade year
because a girl I had a silent crush on
had their poster in her locker.

The way I've picked every scab
I've ever had, over and over
until it's a scar.

All my secrets, safe in Leah's ears
and heart. All of them except
this one.

LEAH IS LOSING PATIENCE BECAUSE I AM LOST IN MY HEAD

so I pull myself together. Sometimes it's hard
to scrape myself off the ceiling of my skull
and pour me into a chair.

But I do. I focus on her face
not her cup
and that's when I see how serious
she is, how her eyes are doing the thing
they do when she's apologizing

in advance. This is how she looked
when she broke up with Brian Jeffries
and had me come with her for moral support—
I'd never seen a boy cry until that day

and he's hated me ever since for knowing.
(Instead he should hate whoever made the rule
that boys aren't supposed to cry.)

But I can't figure out why Leah would be looking at me
like this and I can feel the crocodile in my mind start to shift,
all the possibilities starting to float to the surface of murky water
so I say

   Just say it. Whatever it is, just say it.

And she looks surprised but hesitates for only a moment
before she says
I decided I'm going to DC with Cesar for Young Chemists.

And at first it doesn't register: at first I smile
because she loves Cesar almost as much
as she loves chemistry and Leah has only ever
been to Fort Lauderdale which is barely a real place
and she's always wanted to travel.

But then it sinks in.

Young Chemists is a three-month commitment
and I didn't even know she'd applied.

The realization is like a beanstalk growing out of the table between us
and we both see it,
   the way things have changed,
watching it swell until we can no longer
see each other
at all.

"WHAT ABOUT WILDWOOD?"

And I regret it as soon as it's out of my mouth.
Is this growing up? This flash of melting butter in a pan,
watching something solid turn into steam?
Because when I hear the words
in my voice
and when I see her face
hear them
I realize how childish I sound

like we're still ten
walking through the gates for the first time

pointing at the plush dogs dangling as prizes
licking powdered sugar off our fingers
screaming when the floor of the fun house shifts

and that's how this feels right now:
like the floor has been shifting for the last ten months
and now it has dropped out from under me.

THERE'S NOTHING MORE EMBARRASSING

than realizing that you've been looking
forward to something
alone.

Me and Leah, going to Wildwood
every summer since we were ten.
Turning fifteen and putting in job applications—
blessing from the Ferris wheel gods
when we got hired.

Purple polo shirts and khaki shorts
taking tickets and handling the balloon pop,
setting the bottles back up after the ring toss.

Every night we'd walk to our parents' cars smelling
like popcorn and fireworks smoke.

Leah's arm around my neck,
stumbling through the fun house and flirting
with boys and me still too shy
to talk to girls, Leah whispering *go talk to her*
about the curly-haired girl who worked the darts,

but she was two years older and so I just watched her
all summer like Bambi in the meadow
and it didn't matter because I had Wildwood
and Leah and the constant thrum
of machines and the blur of their bright paint
as they spun.

It wasn't a question of whether we'd apply again,
and the next summer
was even better
me laughing at the face paint booth when Leah came back
from making out with Brian
behind the funnel cake stand, the clown paint
I'd done on her face smeared and weird.

And *this* summer was going to be even better
because it was the last one before senior year
before things got really serious
before things felt too final

and this summer was going to be even better
because I really needed it to be
after the last ten months of a crocodile
somehow slipping into the moat of my brain
    scales always rippling
I really needed it to be
I really needed this

and it only takes one look in Leah's eyes to know
that she's already decided
and worse
that she's not really sorry because something
between us
has already changed.

AT HOME MY DAD HAS LEFT HIS CREDIT CARD ON THE COUNTER

so I can order pizza—he doesn't know
I have his card saved in my phone's wallet.
I've never used it without asking him but sometimes I think about it,
whether he'd notice if I bought a pedicure set I saw on Instagram
or a pair of blue-light glasses I saw a model wearing.
Also on Instagram.

Sometimes the only way to distract myself from the typhoons
    in my head
        from the earthquakes
        from the blizzards
        from the wildfires
            is to dive into the internet headfirst with no snorkel.

I drown in videos of girls putting on flawless makeup
transforming into another person
huskies howling in doorways
people frying Cheetos in skillets

and it works
for a while

but eventually there is a shooting
or a fire
or an earthquake in a part of the country
that doesn't usually have earthquakes
and the ground under my feet is shaking again
and I'm thrown back into the chasm
of my own head.

SOMETIMES I FORGET WE EVER WENT TO CHURCH

until I see the photo here in the kitchen.

Easter, Mandy in a dress and me in a skirt, both half-smiling—
Dad never; Mom always.

Red brick behind us and always between us.

Some families have a wall they can't cross that gets built after
tragedy, trauma. My aunt
and uncle lost their child to a drunk driver and divorced a year
later, barely speak.

For us the wall was always there, invisible and solid.

I don't know who built it or what it's made of; the same way I don't know where my thoughts come from.

So when I consider point of origin, it's safe to infer that the answer is *me*.

I DON'T REMEMBER THE LAST DAY OF CHURCH

but I do remember Mandy whispering in the dark:

Why do you think we don't go anymore?
    Dad wants to open the dojo.

He always said church was how the spirit stays clean.
    Yeah.

Do you think he still believes in hell?
    Of course. Don't you?

I don't know. Maybe now he believes in something worse.

I ORDER INDIAN FOOD INSTEAD OF PIZZA.

What brought us here
to this apartment,
every wall the same
butter yellow
is my parents' pursuit

of a social life, and they found it:
wine tastings, foodie tours.

There are twenty restaurants in a five-block radius
and my parents have been to them all—

with their oldest chick off to college
and me old enough to stay home alone,
they are birds remembering
how to fly.

Sometimes I think they've forgotten
that the nest isn't empty
quite yet.

But even though I'm alone,
Tikka Palace delivers, so close
the delivery guy can walk.

I order vindaloo because the vinegar sauce burns
and I can't take another wildfire in my head or on my phone.

At least in my mouth I can swallow it.

THERE'S ALWAYS LEFTOVERS WITH INDIAN FOOD

because I'm the only one in the house who eats it
since my sister went to college.

I texted her a picture but it's Friday night
and she's doing college things

in Michigan, only posting her nightlife
in Close Friends, which neither
of our parents are techy enough to know exists.
I tap through, smiling at her wrinkled-nose grin,
at the new pink highlights in her hair,

at the green-eyed boy that shows up
in the frame every now and then.

Miranda left in the fall—the only
one I've told
about my thoughts,
the way they streak through my head
    night lightning
painting up everything
white and skeletal. If I closed my eyes
                    (and I won't, because that calls
                    the thoughts up)

I could imagine Mandy creeping over
from her bed across the room. Somehow
she always knew when I was awake.

You okay?

   Yes.

What are you thinking about?

That question.

It took me a long time to tell her.

You're okay. It's not real.

Now she's gone, and the room we used to share
is quiet
except for the times
the prayers I weave like yarn
make it out of my lips:

I'm okay she's okay they're okay.
I'm okay she's okay they're okay.
I'm okay she's okay they're okay.
I'm okay she's okay they're okay.
I'm okay she's okay they're okay.
I'm okay she's okay they're okay.

Six times
    quickly
or it won't work.

Mandy always tells me she misses me,
even though in Close Friends
she's making new friends,
some of them cute,
all of them smitten
with her.

She says she misses me.
I believe her.

But I also think
she's probably at least a little relieved
that she no longer has to share a room with a sister
who sees murder
every time she closes her eyes.

NINE

and church like an iron kernel lodged
in my teeth, tongue worrying it.

If not for Mandy, maybe I would think
more about the Devil. She is a sieve

all my worries about hell pass through,
her metal wire catching all the stones.

I trust my sister like the Bible, even
if I'd never say it out loud.

It isn't Pastor Joe who sees to my nightmares
it's Mandy.

Mandy, the voice in the dark.

Mandy I call out to in the night when
I'm too old for cuddling but need to know
someone is there.

I trust my sister like the Bible
so if she says the Devil isn't real
I believe her

but even Mandy can't answer *why*
do I have these thoughts?
and I guess there are blank spots
in the Bible

where the believer has to carve
out a belief of their own

and I don't remember the first day
we went to church but I do remember
the first *what if:*

moonlight leaking across my windowsill
and the thought unspooling with it

What if the Devil is me?
What if the Devil is me?

MANDY BLAMED CHURCH

I'm glad we don't go anymore. Maybe your nightmares will stay gone.

She was talking about the dream I used to have, every
night like a pointed crescent moon.

Night wake.
Cry out.
Mandy creeping
into my room, before we shared.

Was it the same one?

Hell but not fire. Gray tar
coating my feet. Liquid ash
filthy around my ankles before
it crawled inside my mouth.

   My soul feels dirty.

I don't think souls can get dirty, Ariel.

   That's not what Dad says. What Pastor says.

They're not god. They can be wrong.

WATCHING TV AND ALL THE CARTOON DOGS WEAR MAKEUP

How else are we supposed to know which ones are   girls?
How else are we supposed to know which cat is a   girl
if not for the slight purple tint of her cat eyelids?

In cartoons even animals have boobs
a weird furry shelf of a bust.

Sometimes I imagine aliens from a distant
planet swinging by Earth
taking one glance at our art
and zooming away as they whisper
What the fuck

BEFORE GOING UPSTAIRS

The rule written in blood:

knives.

Tap them all.

Again and again.

Everyone is

    safe.

SOMETIMES WHEN I GET LOST

in social media I find myself
deep in the forest of Instagram,
algorithm leading me
to accounts of girls who have muscles
    lots of them
legs like tree trunks
arms cut like diamonds

and always in the comments
dozens of people saying

You're so pretty—you'd be prettier without all the mass
Don't you want to be more feminine?
At least you're wearing makeup

Sometimes femininity
feels like a maze with nothing
but dead ends.

Don't know how I got in.
Don't know how to get out.

MAYBE A LITTLE EASIER IF YOU HAVE A MOM OR AN AUNT

whose body takes up as much space
as yours. Your existence might
feel like less
of an imposition.

i don't mean to impose
but i have to get by
and you have not left enough
room behind your chair

i know this is inconvenient
but you can move   your chair
and i think the only way i will

ever be smaller
is if i eat the cake that Alice ate
when she crawled through the rabbit hole

The worst part is
I don't want to be smaller
I just want you
to not want
me to be smaller.

Is this a poem to my mother
or is this a poem to myself

self to self
girl to gator
      mouth to itching   ear.

I AM OFF-SCRIPT

Director, producer decided early on
that this character was a girl

Did anyone in the writer's room
stop to ask what that means
what it   really means

because I didn't get the notes

that seem so important to everyone
else. Everyone seems to know
exactly how it feels to be a girl

but when I look around for examples
it's like everyone chose (chose?) the   same one.

Whenever I find a foothold
I feel like I'm in danger of slipping
off—such a narrow pedestal
and my feet are size 12.

I DON'T START WORK UNTIL MONDAY

but on Saturday I walk the six miles
to Wildwood and stand just outside
the gates. Inside they are still unpacking
all the prizes, plush Snoopys and Mickeys,
a million glow-in-the-dark bracelets.

Day by day this summer, those bracelets
will make their way onto the wrists
of everyone in this small-big town, the night
glittering with ritual, fireflies
droning through plastic paradise.

It doesn't smell like popcorn yet—
I only smell oil as they finish greasing
all the greaseable parts of the Tilt-A-Whirl,
the spinning teacups, the tiny slow choo-choo
for the little kids that goes over one hump
and then back down. The emptiness

is because there are no people, but
I can't help but feel it's because even Wildwood

knows that it's missing something essential,
that for it, too, Leah is a vital organ,
everything hollow in her absence.

WHEN MANDY CALLS, SHE ALREADY KNOWS

something is wrong. *You haven't responded*
to my memes. What's up?
and when I tell her, her frown spreads
across my screen. Her first question
after I tell her about Leah is

Are you still going to do Wildwood?
further proof that she can read
at least part of my mind.

She is eating a banana.

                                  Razor blades would slide into it
                                                   so easily.

I just tell her
yes.

THE WORST PART OF MANDY BEING GONE

isn't the empty parts—our room
or the bathroom we used to share
where for the last eight months
I have been free to leave my towel
on the floor and the toothpaste capless.

What if you smashed your mother's teeth with the white marble statue she keeps in her bathroom?

It's the parts that are supposed to feel full.

The dinner table at night
or the fridge in the morning,
me and my parents looking
at each other, almost surprised,
like rare coincidence has brought us

together, two hippos and one tiger
who happened upon the water hole
at the same time. We're all a little
wild, like Mandy was the only thing
keeping us tame, together—a stitch
holding the whole sweater in place.

If Mandy is a stitch
and Leah is a stitch
and both are gone,
how long until
the yarn of me
fully unravels?

ON THE RARE OCCASION MY PARENTS INVITE ME OUT

I usually say yes, because I get sick of eating
at home, even when it's carryout. (Something

about food changes once it crosses the threshold
of your house.) But as soon as I sit down

with my parents at a restaurant, I remember
why I stay home, why I am usually content
to let them go out and leave me alone:

No matter how hot the food is,
it's always cold to my parents.

No matter how fresh the bread is,
it's always stale to my parents.

No matter how charred the meat,
it's always underdone.

Sometimes I wonder if I'm just coincidence,
a foundling that they tripped over
on the way home from the bar.

They would've had to find
Mandy too then, because it was Mandy
who taught me how to tip, and it's a good thing
because when we get up to leave I see
my dad only left 10% so I let them
get to the door before I pretend I forgot
my phone, go back and leave more cash,
mouth *I'm sorry* to the waiter.

I know I'm not like my parents—
they're too happy, too caught up

with whatever it is they're caught up with
to have brains full of blood.

But sometimes I'm grateful.
At least I know
how to tip.

I THINK EVERYONE MY AGE IS EMBARRASSED OF THEIR PARENTS

at least sometimes. Not in the sitcom way
where your parents wear cringe
clothes and the wrong shoes,

but in the ways that are harder to capture
in one frame:

words or worldview,
little thorns that catch on your ear
reminding you of the ways your world
and their world
are square peg and round hole,
the small things that when you look at them directly
get bigger and clearer
like when you twist
the dial on a microscope.

It's the little things I can't let go:
one time we were watching a Marvel
movie just before Mandy left

and my dad said Captain America was his favorite
character, because someone has to be the arbiter
of what is right and wrong
and Mandy said *The Avengers just committed actual war crimes
in Sokovia*

and Dad said *Save it for college*

and I just can't let that go
how when Mandy said
*The white dude who's technically old
thinks he should be the boss of good?*
and Dad said
What's so bad about that?

It was kind of like a splinter under my fingernail

so that every time I reach
for middle ground
it digs a little deeper
and the pain makes me look more closely
at everything else my parents do:

The way they don't ever want to tip
The way they always find a problem that justifies it
The way their smiles fade when the Lyft
driver has an accent on the way home from the restaurant

The way we took a Lyft at all,

when the place
was only five blocks from home
and we could've walked.

But my mom says it's dark
and I wonder why they moved
to a neighborhood they think is too
dark at night
to begin with.

AND THEN THERE'S THE BIBLE VERSES.
Dad knows so many, has read
the Bible so many times,
always has Scripture waiting
on his tongue.

Then why, Mandy would say,
don't you believe in free health care?
Universal basic income?
Why do you have a problem
with the homeless guy
on the corner?

I never joined the arguments—
I never knew what
to say. Mostly I would sit
and juggle all the stuff
he would say about people

who don't deserve
the things Mandy says we all do

and I would wonder
at what point my dad would
eventually look at me
and think the same thing.

MANDY ALWAYS UNDERSTANDS

when I text her, always makes time
for what she left me alone to deal with.

Keep challenging them
she says
They won't change unless you push them

But it's hard to explain how as much as I want to
I don't have the mind that Mandy has,
the way her brain is a blade
that cuts through all the bullshit,
lays it open like a fillet.

This is why she's going to be someone important:
        her thoughts run clear and quick,
        her analysis coming out sparkling.

Conversely, my brain feels like clogged pipes:
        whenever I open my mouth
        all that comes out is rusty water.

Do you ever have the thoughts about mom and dad?
Mandy asks in a text.

    Yes.

You don't think you'd actually hurt them, do you?

    No.

It's not a lie. But it's rusty water.

All I want is to be clear
and clean.

THINGS I DON'T TELL MANDY: A LIST

I don't want to hurt anyone but I think my brain
must,
and who am I
apart from my brain?

I can't go visit Aunt Gina anymore
because she always wants me
to hold the baby. I don't trust
my hands around his fragile
bones.

On Tuesday I stood in the mirror
and slapped my own face
like maybe whatever crept inside me
could be shocked out with the force

but all that happened was my cheek
turning red and Mom asking me
if I'd been asleep on that side.

On Friday night I spent four hours
googling the childhoods
of serial killers, putting their lives
side by side with my own
looking for the tipped domino,
the thing that made them fall apart
so I can find it in my own heart.

Part of me writes this all down
to get it out of my head
        an exorcism in ink
but part of me wants a record
so that if the monster it feels
like I'm becoming ever spreads
through every inch of my skin
and I do what the crocodile
in my brain daydreams
about, that there will be evidence

written in my human hand
that I tried
        I really tried
to stop.

BABIES

Memory: When I was ten, my father's friend asked me what I
wanted
to be when I grew up and I said   *babysitter.*

He laughed: *That's not a job.*

I didn't understand why—my teacher told us you picked a job you
love and I loved
     babies,   sweet

soft things—heads and hands that smelled like milk left in the
bowl after cereal.

Cradle them in your arms and solve all their huge tiny problems.

My cousin's name is Curtis and I haven't held him in three months.
I'm starting to forget

what he smells like.
                 Maybe for the best.

LATELY I CAN'T THINK

about babies without thinking about sex.
The worst part of being a virgin

is having the brain of a not-virgin
and this belongs on the list
of things I don't tell my sister.

Some things are too much for my mouth
to say, they're almost too much
for my hand to write.

This part of my brain is another kind of reptile—
a smooth white snake that slithers
between my eyes when I'm in class or riding the bus.

On the last day of school I was listening
to Mr. Brooks give the farewell speech
and suddenly he was naked.

My brain is like a voyeur for made-up scenarios
peeking into windows that don't exist
and inside the windows was
Mr. Brooks leaning over my bed
reaching for my underwear
and me   reaching back

before I snapped my mind shut,
blowing out the vision like birthday candles.

But the thing about candles is the smoke,
and I couldn't breathe the rest of class
watching him speak and smile while I avoided
the snake in my head
wondering what it meant, wondering how old
he was and what was wrong with me
for fantasizing about a man twice my age
when I don't like men to begin with.

Is it a fantasy if you're not turned on?
Sometimes I squeeze my legs together
under the desk just to check
and I never feel anything.

Why do I never feel anything except
    disgust?

SEX FEELS LIKE A CURTAIN

Standing on this side of not knowing, I can wonder
not just what it will be like but what
I will be like.

Maybe all the thoughts that come
when I least expect them
unsummoned
unwelcome
will fade when I get it over with.

Maybe half the snake
is anticipation.

But pulling back the curtain on sex
will be pulling back the curtain on myself:

if I think like this before I've done it
what will I become after?

It's Sunday night and I want to text Leah and ask
if she's had sex with Cesar yet
if she's going to in DC
does she think she'll feel different after
does she think she'll *be* different.

Everyone always acts like sex
is transformational
but I'm starting to feel like it's not
who
you are that changes, but
what:

the scale in *Willy Wonka*—
Good Egg or
Bad—

the sweet Virgin Mary
or her counterpart in fishnets.

Another thing to be
afraid of.

Once the curtain is pulled back
will I like myself better on the other side,
or will I pass through expecting fewer scales
and instead have grown a tail?

THOUGHTS ABOUT VIRGINITY

In the movies, they never show
girls losing their virginity to other
girls. Almost like virginity
isn't real
unless a boy
is doing
the taking.

Almost like
it's not something
girls do
but something
done to them.

THE FIRST GIRL I FELT LIKE THAT ABOUT

is dead, and she never knew
my name.

I remember hers. Felicia.

Felicia.
Striped shirt.
Backwards cap.

She's gone
from this world
and just like everything else
that's my fault too.

I WAKE UP TO A TEXT FROM LEAH

I hope you have a good summer

and if I didn't know her so well, maybe
it wouldn't hurt so bad
but those seven words are goodbye
and I sink back into my pillow, knowing
it's the last text I will get from her until she returns.

This summer is about the future—Cesar
and college—which means Leah
Scientist Leah
Binary Leah
has relegated me to the past,
at least for a while.

Me and Wildwood are the same rusty
something
and she is tired of oiling my springs.

MANDY WON'T BE HOME FOR THE SUMMER

and I know I shouldn't blame her, she in her escape pod of courses
and an internship at a youth health clinic.

I shouldn't blame her for finding a lifeboat and clinging to it,
waving at me from the shore.

But I'm still on the ship, and the water has reached my knees, and I
shouldn't blame her.

But I do. A little bit. I do.

I ALWAYS THINK OF MY GRANDMOTHER WHEN I PUT ON MY SHOES.

She's gone now, but when I was little
she would press her palm against my cheek
and say *such a good girl.*

I was small and my hair was still that baby-blond
and I hadn't yet started arguing
when my mom laid out dresses
and shiny shoes.

Such a good girl.

I can almost remember the exact day
she began to notice
the change in me

when she stood beside me in her doorway
while I slipped on the shoes
she always made us take off inside.

She noticed my sneakers
while I shoved in my feet
and asked
what size are you wearing?
and I remember the shape
of her frown
when I answered.

THOUGHTS ABOUT SMALLNESS

There was a time when being the biggest was cool.
Fourth grade, back against back, an inch over the boys
might as well have been a foot
long bones strutting.

A brief era of glory. Soon, girls realized
that there was value in being small
     not just *short* but *small*.
Heather Gaines, the shortest girl in fifth grade:
I remember thinking she looked like a baby.

We were so intent on being bigger
                       older
                             farther along.

By eighth grade Heather hadn't grown an inch
and to me she still looked like a child
but suddenly the boys all liked her.

They loved picking her up—
in gym they tossed her to each other like a football
her laughs bigger than her body
     —nicknames like Fun Size.

We were all trying to grow up
and shed baby fat. We
hadn't yet realized that the fat
was the only part we needed
to shed—that there was something

about *baby* that the boys flew to
like bees to spilled soda.

You can hold a baby
You can gather it in your arms
You can teach a baby words
and how to be. You can love
a baby into a particular shape.

If Heather hated being small in fifth grade
she found something to love by ninth,

currency changing with the market,
like thinking the paper in your pocket is trash
until you cross a border and it becomes
a dollar.

DAY 1 AT WILDWOOD

begins.
The gates are open and I step through
holding my breath,

the part of me that is still Disney-fied
from childhood wondering if I'll hear
someone calling my name,
find Leah running across the parking lot,
purple polo waving like a flag.

She will have run all the way from the airport.

But the only person who says my name is Mr. Malcolm,
the old guy with keys on a ring so big it could encircle Saturn.
I still don't know what he does, only that he's allowed to tell me
what to do
and we always say good morning. He says

Good to have you back
and I say *good to be back*
because it's what I'm supposed to say
and I would've meant it if Leah was here.

Pathetic that removing one variable changes
the whole equation, but Leah would say
That's math for you, that's literally the way math works

so I carry on to the office, size 12 feet showing me the way,
two summers committing it to memory,
the sound of the carousel's tune drifting
across the dusty grounds to my ears
and drawing me like a magic spell.

I'm here. My heart's not in it
but my heart has been MIA for ten months
and I've learned to stop wondering when
it will kick back in
and just try to get through the day
without hurting anyone.

IF I'M A CARNIVAL BEAST,
THEN MS. MEGGA IS THE STRONG WOMAN.

She's the kind of woman
who would make my mother's mouth
flatten into a fault line
and I never know if the quake
it conceals is fear or rage—

sometimes the shine in her eyes
looks the same either way.

My mom is the kind of woman
who prides herself on being petite,
like she made a list
of the things women should be
and all of them were synonyms
for small: quiet, nonconfrontational,
pale. (She's learned to make the small
parts of herself sharp:

her quiet voice makes you lean forward
to hear her—Mandy calls this
that passive-aggressive bullshit.)

Ms. Megga is not that kind of woman.

She was a bodybuilder for 15 years,
Mr. Malcolm says,
shoulders that carry Wildwood in the summer
and other worlds I don't even know

about in the offseason, a voice that carries
across the grounds, rattling louder
than the roller coasters. She starts off
every summer as tan as ever

the kind of brown that would make my dad
smile his golf course smile and ask
where's she from and I guess I wonder too
but Cesar said people ask him that
and it makes him feel like a cavity
in a mouth of teeth
so I never ask and instead
blush under the way she tells me
I'm as tall as her son and with broader
shoulders.

From other people, it makes me feel
like Cesar said—a silver cap—
but from Ms. Megga it feels as she intends:
like a crown descending from her heart
to my head.

I USED TO BE STRONGER.

Mr. Cipinko started weight-lifting club after school
and it met the same day as Young Chemists.

I have never been flush with extracurriculars—
Mrs. Madison the college advisor already

planting yellow flags of warning on my
twisting path toward graduation.

I went expecting nothing and instead found
a man whose forehead met my shoulder,
small-boned and sharp-eyed
with his wrists wrapped in black.

Mr. Cipinko taught the seniors
so I hadn't had him yet, but he showed me
how to lift with my legs and drop my butt

how to let the muscle and not the joint
curl the weight. Relax your neck, let your body
do the work it wants to do.

I lifted weights on Tuesdays and Thursdays
for nine weeks until the football guys
changed their schedule, and also maybe until
my mother started pointing out the size
of me, growing like a pupil in darkness. I realized
that some people lifted weights to feel strong
and some lifted weights to feel powerful

which is sometimes the same thing
and sometimes isn't.

"YOU LOOK LIKE A GUY"

Muscles don't look good in dresses

Don't you want curves

Dude, you're like a dude

Muscles aren't feminine

    But I don't wear dresses

    No

    No

    But I don't want to be feminine

    Or do I?
    Otherwise why
    does any of this
    needle under my skin

    why does any of this
    bother me at all?

I never know what I'm trying
to be.

I just want to be
    right.

MEGGA HAS JUST BEGUN CATCHING ME UP

when the door of her office swings open,
the smell of cinnamon
apples sweeping in with motor oil,
dust like tiny silver bubbles
before a wave, and when it clears

there's a girl:

almost as tall as me
but not as broad
braids spilling down around her face
lavender at the tips,
dark skin shiny with sweat.

In the second it takes for her vision
to adjust in the dim office
I've already sized her up—

the purple Converse
the long cargo shorts, white
tank top, collarbones like a shelf
below her throat. Then her eyes
clear and she sees me, fake-
smiles before she says to Ms. Megga
Good morning, y'all hiring?

and if I'm actually a carnival beast,
for a moment everything with fangs
inside me
takes a breath
and purrs.

I KEEP STARING AT HER

while Ms. Megga starts her speech,
the one I heard when me and Leah
had applied that first year:
Wildwood only takes referrals, carnival
work is different from other jobs,
it requires a little bit weird
and a little bit wild and Leah,
because she's good at this
because she was destined
for college interviews,
convinced Megga we were born
for carnival work,
that we'd spend every day
at Wildwood even if we didn't work
here, because we grew up in the neon,

in the fortune-telling booths,
in the crash and screech
of bumper cars,
we dreamed in cotton candy . . .
and Ms. Megga had laughed
and told her to shut up
that we were hired
because she knew our faces
and knew it would work out.

But I know with one glance
that the girl with the braids

doesn't have a referral,
that she's never been to Wildwood
to begin with. Her eyes are bunny-
wide, taking in the photos on Megga's
walls, the history of Wildwood
snapped in black and white—
the girl is an asteroid that has plummeted down
and found herself here

and for some reason it makes me
interrupt Ms. Megga's speech
and lie
because I guess I've gotten so good
at lying that I do it when it's not needed
and I say
It's okay, Ms. Megga, I know her.
You can give her Leah's job.

THE GIRL'S NAME IS RUTH

and she smiles at me sideways
when Ms. Megga gives her a purple polo
after a few other questions.

Ms. Megga radios Mr. Malcolm
and he comes to give Ruth the tour

while Megga finishes telling me
about what my new assignment is.

You were pretty good last summer,
she says, and when I raise
my eyebrow
she points at the top of the sketchbook
poking out from my bag.
Have you gotten better?

She asks me to show her my sketches
and then she smiles.

We're going to do
something new.

AT MIDNIGHT I FLIP THROUGH MY SKETCHBOOK

All day, instead of taking tickets or setting up fallen bottles
Ms. Megga had me fluttering
from ride to ride like a pigeon,
sketchbook in hand
to draw portraits of Liam, at the Ferris wheel
Taurean, at the bumper cars
Ms. Linda, making funnel cakes
(though I leave out her silver flask).

As many people as would sit still.

You know how to make paper
become a face. With this,
try to see the things you think

54

they see about themselves
and make that the brightest
thing on the page.

Megga was talking about portraits:
this summer, she wants me
drawing caricatures three times a week,
a new thing for Wildwood she dreamed up
in the offseason.

Next summer I'll get you an airbrush,
she said, *so we can do color.*

Her vision for Wildwood automatically has me in it
and even if I wanted to argue, any alternate plan
is made of cotton candy at this point:
spun out of sugar, barely there,
dissolving in rain.

So instead I listened while she gave me
tips for learning caricature:
shading and shape,
expression,
and I asked her
Did you use to be an artist?

and she smiled in that way
that makes people call her Mystery Meg
and said
Sweetie, what haven't I been
in this life?

I LOOK AT THE FACES

that now live in my notebook:
Ms. Linda's mouth tugging at the corners
and the new kid stationed
at the carousel, the way his eyes

arrow sideways on the page
because he could never look right at me
for more than a few seconds.
Mr. Malcolm and his gap, his bushy eyebrows.

Every line always feels like an accident
until they begin
to come together, and I'd been nervous
drawing strangers
at first
but now here in my room I see the way
I got little details so right
they seem to glow.

But more important than the lines
is the realization I have at 12:55am
when I eventually decide
I should probably sleep:

that I'd gone the whole day
drawing faces
and not a second
imagining them
dead.

IT'S LIKE A DIET,

starving yourself all day
and when you get home
then close the door

all the cabinets
        open themselves
as your mouth
        fills with the saliva
            it's been swallowing in the daylight.

A diet turns you
into a werewolf
and the beast in my brain
is no different:

a long day of keeping the thoughts away
means the crocodile is starving
for them at night.

It doesn't matter if I hate the moon.
It doesn't matter if I hate the green water.

My bed is not a safe place.

It seems like the longer I try to starve this
the hungrier it gets.

ALL THE ARTICLES ABOUT SERIAL KILLERS
want to know why,
search for explanations.

Of course they do:

everyone wants to stop them
or at least to make sense
of what the headlines call senseless:
    order to the universe
    prayer of protection

I've learned a lot about gray matter
since trying to understand myself:
many serial killers, the research says,
have less of it in the front of their brain
    (or something)
and it doesn't *make* them kill
but it makes them unable to stop
and I haven't figured out if that's the same thing.

What's clear is that almost without exception
these people had horrible childhoods
    people who hurt their bodies and their minds
    people who were supposed to take care of them
    and didn't/couldn't: family
    and foster homes
and because our society is full of holes
that lead to even deeper holes,
the people with holes in their brains
just slide down and down and down

until there's nothing to catch them
but blood.

My parents have never laid a hand on me—
this should make me feel better.

I have no idea what my gray matter looks like—
if it's Swiss cheese or as solid and whole as poured steel

but the blood is there either way.

I have no excuse
for everything that happens in my brain.

No reason
that I can remember, only two normal if distant parents
a bed to sleep in, food to eat

No reason for feeding myself with nightmares
or sleeping in swamps.

If you've had a bad life
and have holes in your head
        you need help—

but if you're like me
I can't help but think
        you just need hell.

I WATCH VIDEOS UNTIL I PASS OUT

and the algorithm must have read my mind because I end up
on dietitian TikTok where I learn
that there's no such thing as a diet
that's not actually disordered eating
in disguise.

Even though it's 3am
part of me wants to wake up my mother
shake her awake with the phone shining in her eyes

then maybe we can clear out all the cookbooks,
the angular faces of their authors taking up all the space
on the windowsill blocking the light
to the mini herb garden.

It's not only the time that keeps me in my room
but the knowledge
that it's pointless:

if the whole world is Wildwood, my mother
is on the carousel, around and around to tinny music,
and I'm not on a ride at all.

I watch her from outside the gates
wondering why
she's such
a clown.

CASE IN POINT:

When we inevitably collide in the kitchen at 8:30am
my father is getting ready for karate
and my mother is holding a plate
of sliced kiwi.

She looks at my bowl of granola
plus toast
and says
That's a lot of carbs.

Her new thing is eating only fruit
before noon
and I just stare at the banana
in her hand
still unpeeled.

She's proud of these decisions,
feels like she's getting away
with something if she makes it to twelve o'clock
without eating anything at all.

I've learned that some spaces between us
are fragile ground:

I am six inches taller than her
thirty-five pounds heavier

and I don't think she's realized
that I am a separate human

and not merely a bigger,
wronger version
of her.

My bigness is a violation of the secret pact
she has with "small"
and at some point I'll stop caring
but it's not today.

WHAT IS IT ABOUT ACNE

that can ruin your whole day? I think you're a liar
if you say you can scroll by endless poreless faces
and not have the flat perfection leak into your eyeballs,
seep into the blood and to your brain.

My mom says she grew up on magazines
and social media is better—
she used to spend her whole allowance on the gloss
-y pages and you can see it all for free now:

celebrity workouts and their favorite shampoo

digital Bible.

The only thing magazines have on social,
she says, is that you could cut the magazines out
tape them to your door and to the mirror

Wish wall she calls it. I don't tell her
about all the TikTok videos where girls talk
about "manifesting" vacations to Spain and Thailand.
My mom does just fine on her own.

I don't have a wish wall. My bedroom looks empty
now that it's mine, and not me and Mandy's.

Her side was always wallpapered with atlases,
botanical diagrams, not because she even was interested
in botany but because the lines were so gentle, she said,
and the handwriting so neat and curved.

She was the kind of kid always thinking
about what she wanted to be, then changing her mind.
Every color was her favorite. Too many things.

Mandy, always trying to find a way toward
her many dreams. And me, just trying
to find a way.

MEN ONLY HIT ON ME WHEN I'M SITTING DOWN

Coffee shop
Bus
Library
Ticket tent
Movie theater

It's like when my legs unfold
and I stand up
        and keep going up
I am both beanstalk
and giant
and men are usually more interested
in golden geese.

A giant needs a sword to be felled
and men don't typically carry swords
anymore—

it makes me wonder what they were hungry for
in the first place
if the thing that makes them lose their appetite
is something not easily conquered.

MY IPHONE WON'T LET ME FORGET

the first summer I worked at Wildwood—
new photo memory popping up on my screen
and shaking loose like a shelf of ice from a berg:

me and Leah in those purple polos,
me with teeth freshly freed from braces
and not quite sure how to smile without them.

Before she met Cesar,
before she started her internal
college countdown,
the future like a spacecraft

she will inevitably be beamed up
inside. But for me

the future exists on a very different
plane. It's not that I don't think about
what is to come, it's that all my imaginings
of tomorrow
are dripping red what-ifs:

What if we get nuked while I sleep
Could we find a basement close enough to avoid a tornado
What if I have cancer and don't realize until it's too late
What if our house burns down

What if I set the fire?

I'M RUNNING THE FERRIS WHEEL

when I hear Mr. Malcolm cussing at Jason.
There's a specific way old men cuss that sounds
soft and hard at the same time:
every *motherfucker* sounds like a sledgehammer
but in between is *now you listen here*
so you never really know
just how serious things are.

But Jason's eyes are wide
and as Mr. Malcolm's assistant he knows him
well enough to know when to shut up
so he does

and all I can hear is

Now you listen here you little rat-tailed
motherfucker
if that boy wants to be called a boy
then you will call him what he wants
to be called,
you don't hear me arguing with you
when you call yourself a ladies' man
you weak-chinned
bastard

and I've never actually noticed Jason's chin
but he disappears before I can really look
and by then Mr. Malcolm realizes people can hear him
and he vanishes too in a jingle of keys.

I let the next wave of people board the Ferris wheel
and the next time I look the only person I see
is the new kid,
whose face I sketched yesterday,
not yet name-tagged, and just like yesterday
he catches my eye
before his gaze bounces
back out to the sky.

TEXTS WITH MY SISTER

Mandy: have you heard from Leah?
Mandy: . . .

Mandy: are you ignoring me or the question?

Ariel: I've been at work

Mandy: you always text at work

Ariel: no I haven't heard from her. She's in DC.

Mandy: that doesn't mean she can't text

Ariel: I think it does actually

PARENTS SET THEMSELVES UP FOR FAILURE

by giving their kids names that mean too much.
Some people put so much weight
in names, and how is a baby
supposed to carry
anything so heavy
as their parents' dreams?

My mother wanted sons
but got us instead
then looked to Shakespeare
for what to call us

and settled on *The Tempest,*
which neither of them must have read.

Or maybe people don't care
what a character does or did
when it's Shakespeare,
only that when someone asks
they can say
it's Shakespearean.

It's funny to me
reading Miranda as the dutiful daughter
oblivious to the evils of the world
when the Mandy I know talks about
colonialism at the dinner table
in between bites of seared tofu.

But I know my parents didn't actually read
The Tempest and maybe no one
actually does
because why would you invite
the storm-bringing spirit
into your home if you could help it?

Either way,
they did.

THERE ARE ALWAYS GROUPS OF BOYS AT WILDWOOD

roaming like something not quite wolves—
maybe dogs who, at home
are domesticated but   outside
of the yard and into the company
of their kind   forget everything
they're supposed to know—

they howl and snap
and when they come
to the Ferris wheel to give

me their tickets
they push and jostle
and I've seen it all before:

They will either all board together
and then rock the cart
to identify who among them feels fear

or they will board individually
and shout at each other
across empty space.

They are noise and movement
and constantly measuring each other.

It feels exhausting
even from the outside,
but when they get off
and tell me *thanks, man*
and crow with laughter
I think that while it must
be exhausting to be inside
whatever ritual they're performing—
on the hunt for something
to sacrifice,
always prowling for goats—

that's nothing compared
to how it feels to be
the thing being sacrificed.

I am tired of bleeding.

And bleating.

THREE HOURS WORKING THE FERRIS WHEEL

makes me think about the sky,
watching the people high up,
the brave ones rocking the car
the horny ones making the most
of the time at the unseen top

but all of them framed by the bald blue
expanse of summer ceiling,
the occasional seagull finding its way inland and
scavenging for cheese fries.

Wildwood is always busy and it's because
this whole place
feels like flying, brief and hot
like summer itself

and something about the carnival
feels like being seventeen—

how the daytime is an open-mouthed grin
with hands in the air and tongues stained
red with cherry ice.

But when the sun goes down and the neon
crackles to life
those red tongues find shadows
where they meet the neck
of the girl you saw earlier
as she tossed darts in short shorts,

day and night orbiting each other
until they crash together
in an explosion of fire and sound
like the fireworks they set off
alongside the moon
on the last night before Wildwood closes
for the season.

Wildwood has been open since before I was born
but Wildwood is seventeen

or maybe it only feels that way
because I am too.

IN THE AFTERNOON I'M PRACTICING FACES AGAIN

Megga interrupting my break to present me
with fancy markers and a sketch pad
the size of a computer screen.
Your materials, she says.
By next week you need to be good

enough to start taking money.
Got it?
You can keep your tips.

I've never made money from art before—
my doodles, like my daydreams,
have become increasingly
more elaborate
but
    also like my daydreams
tucked away from the eyes of the world.

Thinking about drawing in public
makes me anxious
    what-ifs starting to unspool
but it's daylight and that means brain-diet
and I push them down

go from ride to ride
to sketch more Wildwood employees:

Brian at the balloon pop
who frowns like an Easter Island head
while I sketch because he's still bitter
that I saw him cry. I can tell he wants to ask
where Leah is and I'm glad he hates me
too much to give in.

Stella twisting cotton candy
around cones, kids with hungry eyes
watching her spin it like a magic spell.

I'm starting to get better.
I'm starting to notice the features
that can be made larger and more dramatic
without making anyone ugly:
Stella's big square veneers
and the tilt of her head when she delivers
sweetness into waiting hands.

My brain is so focused
on the movements of my fingers
that it rocks the crocodile right
to sleep.

"WHAT ABOUT ME?"

It's almost dusk and my hand
is a cramped claw
my sketchbook full of new faces
but Ruth is calling to me from the ticket booth.

I'd almost forgotten about her
but as soon as I see her again
I wonder how:

the sun is setting behind the booth
where she leans out the small window
elbows on the counter
and it's like the orangesicle glow
is melting out from her smile.

Her eyes sparkle like anime,
like she's looking at clear water
running over rock, and I'm relieved
that the current is running fast enough
to hide the mud at the bottom.

WHEN I DRAW RUTH

I take my time. I've learned
how something human
can emerge from a scattering of nothing
and I don't even know Ruth's last name
but I learn her

in the time it takes to form
her high forehead
on the paper, her eyes
that are almost too big for her face;

to create her front teeth
and the gap between them
her tongue peeking out pink and curious
when she smiles;

in the time it takes to draw
the short fine hair along her hairline,
how it's been swooped
into cursive ripples, all the way
down to her sideburns—

I have learned her face,
and when I finally pause and
really look up,
find her looking back,
I realize she has
learned mine too.

"YOU'RE GOOD"

she says.
She's talking about my drawing
but I can't hear *good*
anymore
without the echo of its opposite

like the sweep and slide
of reptilian scales
in a hallway of my brain.

I can't say thank you because
it feels like accepting the compliment
she didn't mean to give,

and I may be a monster
and I may be a liar
but I don't want to be that kind
of liar, the one
who hears *you are good*
and agrees long enough
to sneak inside the cracked door.

WHAT IS IT ABOUT A CARNIVAL

that makes everything less real? Sometimes I feel like Wanda—
Scarlet Witch hiding in a reality of my own making:

the balloon pop and the plush purple unicorns,
                              cinnamon and sawdust.

I am in a room padded with memories. Even before Leah
removed herself to DC, this had become a place that felt secure:

    nostalgia like a cellar I hunker down inside
    while the storm rages on the other side
    of the concrete.

But I'm not Wanda, or a witch,
because if I were, the padded room wouldn't have boys
like the one that talked to me today, he and his friends
waiting for me to let them on the bumper cars.

How tall are you?

    5'11"

You can't be—I'm 6'2"

    I know how tall I am.

I could never date a tall girl.

    Good thing I don't want to date you.

Jesus, what size shoe do you wear?

> *Please wait for all the cars to come to a stop before removing your*
> *seat belts.*

Lift the bar, open the gate—boys my age, and some college guys,
stampede past, yelling, pushing.

Sometimes talking to people feels like I accept more than words—
like the conversation is a physical thing I could put on a scale and
weigh—small but dense.   Then I carry it.

I watch the boys—manhood inertia
      zooming around the metal floor, their laughter louder than the
      crash of car against car.

The boy who spoke to me has hair the color of a bird's nest,
eyes like windows in winter. I wonder what he carries from the
conversation while he speeds back and forth.
                                    Anything?

From this distance, I might finally look small to him.

He looks the same to me. His chin lifted to meet my gaze.

I know how tall I am.

SOMETHING ABOUT ME BEING TALL BRINGS OUT THE VENOM IN MEN.

Even grown ones, shouldering past me in grocery stores
standing on my feet in line at the movies.

How tall are you?—always with a tone like suspicion
and for some reason they almost always say they're 6'2"
                          (even though I never ask)

like this is some magic number that will grant them
      some imagined prize
will enter them in a lottery that can only be won
      by people who are exactly 74 inches tall.

The length of my spine, my arms and my legs
flip a switch: *I am 6'2"* they say
                          (even though I never ask)
even as I'm staring down
at their bald spot.

Something about my body is a broken promise
and even though I don't know how
it became my problem
I'm always wanting to apologize.

SUMMER NIGHTS ARE ENDLESS AND EMPTY

Last year I would have hung around Wildwood
sitting on the rails with Leah
and laughing at the sky

but now I let my feet carry me past my neighborhood
and up to Longroad, the strip of nightlife
where people older than my parents
have their date nights
walk on the promenade
and drink under string lights.

It's full of the kind of restaurants
that look exhausting to sit inside,
art galleries filled with landscapes
all imagined the same way.

But what makes Longroad
worth the trip
is the movie theater:

Fine 5—

low-ceilinged, poorly lit
mostly playing movies that were made
before I was born. Five theaters
with smaller screens than regular theaters
but they still have popcorn and candy
and the floors are still sticky from spilled sodas
and one of the theaters still smells like smoke
from a fire that also happened
before I was born.

It was Leah who learned
that the back door is always open
and it's only four o'clock so no one would notice

if I went around back and slipped inside—
we didn't pay for one movie all last summer.

But with all the lying I do all day long
pretending to be a normal person
lately I've taken every excuse to be honest
about the things
I'm able to be honest about.

So I go the ticket counter and dig
$5 out of my pocket because I hate
purses, point at the showing of *Ocean's Eleven*
and ask the woman at the counter
how much to stay and watch all five movies?

And she squints at me over the counter
tells me that the last showing doesn't let out until 11:45
and when I shrug she tilts her head,

then reaches out and stamps my hand
with a red smiley face and says
Just go on ahead.

IN REGULAR THEATERS, THEY CARE IF YOU BREAK YOUR NECK:
light strips down the aisles so you can see
if you need to pee
or flee

but Fine 5 is so dark
that everything except
    the screen
    and the emergency exit
ceases to exist

    my knees
disappearing into the dark
    my hands and
    their bitten nails
everything fades to black
even   (for a while)
    the thoughts in my head.

ANOTHER REASON

I prefer
Fine 5 is
because
unlike
other
theaters
the aisles
are wide

room
to
extend.

Here,
I am
allowed
to be
long.

There
is space
for me
here
in the
dark.

JOKE'S ON ME.

A casino heist created a false sense of security
and I stepped into the next movie
without looking at the banner
and by the time it really got going
it was too late.

American Psycho
where a rich white guy in a suit is killing
basically everybody.

By the time we get to the scene
where he's dropping a chain saw
down a flight of stairs

my crocodile is already awake, its tail thrashing
in the murky water of me
my thoughts spiraling as if around a drain

and as I stare up at the screen
everything around me dark
I run up against the question that always arises
when I watch movies like this:

is the feeling of dread that claws at my stomach
because I'm looking at something terrible
or is it because something terrible
is looking out of me
and seeing itself?

THE BATHROOM AT FINE 5 IS OUT OF A HORROR MOVIE TOO

Small and old, lime-green tile and grout gray with age. Three
stalls, none big enough for a wheelchair; the soap dispenser
always empty. It's that kind of place and it's not fine
but when is anything ever?

When I go in between shows, there's a woman and her
teenage daughter washing their hands—water
only, I assume. It's not until

I go to flush that I realize they're still there,
and the mother is talking about me.

This sort of thing just shouldn't be allowed.
This is the ladies' *room. Did that look like*
a lady to you?
I don't think so.
I don't know why

they have to try this sort of thing
in public. Keep it at home.
There could be children here.

It's not the first time for this. But
I can tell they're waiting and it's
the first time for that.

I want to stay here forever, with the lime-green tile
at my elbow and the smell of antiseptic
making me dizzy. It's all better than what's
out there.

I flush again, wishing it would take me down
too, and when I step outside the stall
I know I was right.

What do you think you're doing? she says. Her daughter
looks like she too wishes
she could flush herself away.

Everything I start to say feels like an apology.
She won't let me begin.

This bathroom is for girls, the woman says.

    I know.

Then why are you in here?

    I am a girl.

It's not about what you think *you are. It's about
what you* actually *are.*

How do I tell her that there's no bathroom
for what I think I am?
Stick figures, one with legs, one with a triangle
dress. I need another with horns.

I just need to wash my hands.

You should be ashamed of yourself, she tells me.

Mom, let's go

You should be ashamed of yourself!

It's not until they're gone that I whisper
to the mirror: *I am.*

WALKING PAST THE DOJO

I sometimes get glimpses of my father, never
at the front of the class but instead
either straight back in the office
or hovering at the edge of the mat
studying the flurried lines,
children in white gis.

He never interjects—*Jeff knows
what he's doing,* he says. But knowing
my father like I do, I see the stiffness

of his mouth that gives away his awareness
of a lack. Something is missing
here, something only he will notice.

The whole world is always falling
short of a standard that only he can measure.

It would be easier to hate him for it
if he enjoyed it. But if we have anything
in common, it's that things are never quite right
even when we really want them to be.

I STAY UP UNTIL 4AM GOOGLING SERIAL KILLERS.

By now I know most of their names
and as I scroll through the things they did
the bodies found and not found
I look for the same details I always do:

Did they fight it?
Did the knife, the axe, the rope
materialize in their head
inescapable and magnetic?

But by now this is ritual
and I know what I'm going to find:

angry men, almost always white,
who strangled cats as adolescents
who left crime scenes with erections

and even though none of it makes me feel good—
    the chalk lines and the testimonies—
it does accomplish what it always accomplishes:

I close my eyes knowing
that something may be wrong with me
but I'm not like that.

I'm not like
that.

NO, I'M SOMETHING ELSE

I'm worse
worse
worse

> **What made you think
> you could sleep**
>
> **after what you've done?**

What
have I done?

> **So many things
> so many that you can't keep count—**
>
> **don't you remember?**

And that's the worst
part

(if there is a worst
of the worst)

the certain doubt:

certain that I'm forgetting
something

that there is blood
I've drawn and don't remember

that I am walking through life
struggling to stay innocent

when I'm already
guilty
as sin.

I
don't
sleep.

ONE THING I'VE LEARNED FROM SEEING SO MANY MOVIES
is that girls can do anything.

Girls can
    be president
marry princes
    walk the catwalk

go to Harvard
    have sex
drink beer
    climb mountains
punch people
    wear high heels
punch people
    have sex
dance
    sing onstage
swing baseball bats
    shoot people
join the army
    fly airplanes
arrest people

There are so many things we can do and be

so, comparatively speaking,
the list of things we can't be seems so short
    so reasonable.

According to the movies we cannot be:
fat
taller than the (male) love interest
or
old

and only very rarely can we be:
not white
not straight
not cis

We can be anything
We can be so many things

We can be so many things
as long as they're
in the script.

FIRST NIGHT SHIFT OF THE SUMMER

and I'm reminded of the way the carnival changes faces
when night starts to fall
the way the children and their parents filter out,
arms wrapped around stuffed llamas
and popcorn in their teeth

then slowly Wildwood fills up with
everyone who comes to laugh loud
and scream curses from the Tilt-A-Whirl.

The tattoo booth opens,
the window for the beer booth goes up,
and the music drifting out of the fun house shifts into hard rock.

Wildwood closes at midnight but Megga
always ends the girls' shifts at 9—
The freaks come out at night
and everyone knows the freaks
    the real ones
never really go away
but she has a point:

Maybe a different kind of trip then,
he says, and moves off,
dragging broom and dustpan

and even after the group from the fun house comes out
falling all over themselves
alive
unburnt
I keep watching Rex
who even though he's not looking at me
makes me feel a little too seen.

SOMETIMES I CAN FEEL IT GATHERING

like being in the sun too long, the burn
drawing itself slowly on my skin.
But other times it's sudden.
Lightning strike:
dead body, empty sockets,
the eyes bleeding in my palms—
the crocodile is creative,
I'll give it that.
I've never been one for horror
movies and that makes it even worse:
the material materializing
from nowhere, but the burning
white explosion
happening 24 hours a day,
too bright to look at directly
but illuminating my entire life
either way.

I DON'T WANT TO TEXT MANDY

because lately I'm aware
of how much of a burden
I had become before she left,
how many hours of sleep she probably missed
with me tossing and turning across the room.

She deferred college for a year
and I know it was because of me.

But I text her anyway
because my hands won't stop shaking
until I do, my heart won't stop hammering:

Mandy, do you ever think about killing people?

But I stare at the words on my screen, imagine them
zipping through cyberspace into my sister's phone . . .

What if
     when eventually I hurt someone
the police look through her phone and see this message,
then arrest her for aiding and abetting?

All Mandy has ever wanted to do is go
to college, all she has ever wanted
is to get out of our father's house and stretch her wings.

Who am I to clip them, crocodile jaws
smashing through every perfect bone?

In the end, I delete the message,
backspacing even after the screen
is clear. No trace of the things in my head,
everything locked away.

Deep inside, I hear the crocodile
sigh in contentment, because
even though Mandy always reassures me—

you are not a bad person
I think you're normal
there's nothing wrong with you—

the fear always saws a hole in the floor
in a perfect circle around my feet.

Mandy has always soothed me—
she is an angel's whisper in the dark.

But what about when the time comes
where even she can't argue with the yellow eyes
glowing from my soul?

What happens when I ask
am I okay
and the only thing left for her to say is   *no?*

SOMETHING ABOUT MANDY MAKES IT WORSE

and better.

It's hard to explain.

If I'm treading water in a swamp
and I think the crocodile is lurking somewhere beneath

I reach out my hand to Mandy

Am I okay
Am I okay
Am I okay

And she tells me yes
I am okay
I am okay
I am okay

In the moment
it pulls me up out of the sludge—
I am safe.

Everyone is safe.

But the next time it happens
when the swamp water brims at my chin
I need her again.

I need her again and again

and sometimes it feels like those water wings
that people put on their kids—
inflatables around my shoulders and chest.

Bobbing along
held up by artificial air
instead of learning to swim.

But who swims in a swamp?
Who has a prayer
of coming out free and clean
when they're swimming in a swamp?

So I reach for Mandy
again and again
again and again

I reach for Mandy so many times
it's a ritual—
I reach for Mandy
every time
even though she's hundreds of miles away
and trying to live a swampless life.

I can't help it.
I have to.

She's one of the ways I keep
everyone safe.

I HADN'T CONSIDERED THE SIX MILES HOME AT NIGHT.

Without a car, going home on the bus
was the only option and now the bus
is not an option either.

The dark makes it worse.
Fewer witnesses, the reptile says
even when I shush it.

I roam Wildwood, watching
the couples: hand in hand, tossing
balls for bears. My parents
are on a date like this,
drinks with friends.

I could call them
but it would be a whole thing.

*Shouldn't you be doing an internship
instead of that dingy carnival?*

*Is this job worth walking
twelve miles round trip?*

Someone is waving at me—Ruth.
The purple polo brings out the blue
in her skin. I shouldn't go over.
Who knows what I'll do.

But her smile is magnetic
and I'm nothing if not
cold metal.

RUTH IS WORKING THE DART TOSS

taking wrinkled tickets and stuffing them
into the dusty apron around her hips.

She hands the darts across the booth,
winking at a little kid as she slips him
four instead of three.

One, two, POP, POP.

One blue dog, Ruth crows,
and someone hands her
the prize. It's Rex, I realize:
he's blowing up her balloons,
passing her prizes.

We all talk between customers,
not knowing each other well enough
to do much but people-watch,
and that's the great thing about Wildwood:

there is so much to see that you don't have to
look at yourself. You can watch the pigeons,
the occasional rat making off with popcorn,
someone getting a lap dance on the Ferris wheel,

a girl waltzing with a giant stuffed llama
she won at the bottle rings,
someone filming a TikTok in front of the fun house
take 4, 5, 6

What are you supposed to be here but bizarre?
What sounds are you supposed to make
except winning crows and roller coaster screams?

When Jason and his friends wander by
the neon paints them pleasant pink—
it's not until they're closer that I change my mind.

Aren't you ladies supposed to be off at 9?
They're talking to me and Ruth but
they're especially talking to Rex,

who is stapling a balloon to the wall
up high where Ruth can't reach.
He's good at ignoring noise
that wants to hurt him.

Ruth is frowning but silent
and then it happens:

I feel like I'm in fourth grade
screaming *fuck* at a boy on the school bus.
I can't ride buses anymore
and I'm not small anymore either

I'm as tall as Jason and I feel spit leave my lips
when I scream at him.

My phone is slipping out of my hand
I hear it shatter

then Mr. Malcolm is jogging up and shouting at Jason
and waving his hands at me like he's shooing a raccoon

Ruth is scream-laughing and has her hand around my bicep,
she and Rex dragging me off
leaving Jason and my phone behind, escaping
toward the parking lot

where we (three) drive away.

RUTH STEERS THE CAR THROUGH TACO BELL'S DRIVE-THRU

and orders an armada of tacos.

I don't know if she and Rex are talking
because my head is so full of noise—

throat raspy from screaming
hands shaking . . .

What happened to the darts?

They had been in my hand,
tossing them back and forth
while people-watching—

**What did I do with them? Did I drop them? Did I
jab them into Jason's thigh? They were right in
my hand, I was the only one on the same side of
the counter. Did I hurt him? The moments reverse
and forward, reverse and forward. His blue eyes,
his dark lashes, wide in shock. I stabbed Jason.
All of it runs together. Dart in thigh, in cheek, in
eye. Blood as red as the plastic fletching...**

—crocodile chomping its teeth

It feels like the only way
to keep people safe is to stay away from them,
a gap wide enough for all the thoughts to fall into.
Did I hurt him? I ask, and they both laugh.
They don't know I'm really asking.

I'm glad Mr. Malcolm came, Ruth says.
I thought you were going to beat that kid's ass.

I need to ask: *Did I hurt him? Did I stab Jason with those darts? Just
one? Both?*

How can I?

Asking means not knowing.
Not knowing means I am out of control.
Out of control means people get hurt.

I WASN'T ALWAYS LIKE THIS.

I can remember going to sleep without counting
the prayers, I can remember *Good night, Mandy*
floating like winter breath,
the syllables free and unexamined.

Sometimes it feels like I'm possessed,
like one day I was passing a haunted house
and something made the leap
from the attic of the building
to the attic of my skull.

But when I really think about it
whatever is in me has always been there—
little glimpses of the green scales:

a sleepover in third grade
when the host's dad put on a mask
and knocked on all the windows.

Everyone screamed and hid
and giggled but all I could do
was be silent and imagine
the bodies of my friends
laid out around the living room
like open-eyed dolls.

A third grader shouldn't think
like that.

But I always have, fleeting
thoughts I knew were wrong
that mired me in sticky guilt.

But it wasn't always like *this,*
the sticky feeling transforming
from spilled soda to fast-drying
cement, my brain
getting stuck in blood
instead of mud . . .
returning to the thoughts
while eating cereal,
while roller-skating.

Sometimes they submerge—
when I stay busy and talk a lot
I can keep them at bay
at least until I get in bed
and they flood my head like fire ants.

But since Mandy left
it's been harder,
and with Leah gone
it feels like
        little by little
blood is a swamp
I sink into

and as Ruth turns
the car into the park,
I'm positive

that if she knew
the contents of my head
she would have left me
at the carnival
with Jason.

THE RIVER LOOKS LIKE OIL IN THE NIGHT

and even in the dark, boats slide west
toward the twinkling lights of the port.

When Ruth parks the car, she sits still
for a long moment, scanning the waterfront,
before opening the car door. Rex and I
follow, all the way
across the grass to a graffitied picnic table
where Ruth dumps the tacos like a net of bass.

They're all chicken, she says. *Everyone
likes chicken.*

This feels like a dream.

We eat. I'm quiet.
In the air between us: Jason's face,
the wideness of his eyes.
I can feel them giving me space.

Wouldn't they tell me if I stabbed him?
Wouldn't they be saying *how could you?*

Then Ruth holds up a sauce packet, peering
at the little phrase Taco Bell has printed on it:

If you never do, you'll never know,
she reads.

Rex follows suit:

I'm in good hands now.

I'm afraid to read one—what if somehow
the words are something terrible, transform
before I realize it and say them out loud?

But they're looking at me, so I carefully select
a packet and hold it toward the light:
Be gentle, I say softly.

Ruth looks straight at me
Too late, she says, teeth shining again
and it's so funny and scary

I snort-laugh a tomato to the back
of my throat and when Rex
thumps my back it goes flying out
into the dark.

What a night, Ruth sighs,
like she's been on a romantic walk
like she's been gazing at stars
like she's been dancing in moonlight

and with the threat of the tomato gone
I laugh and laugh, the way a hyena
might—like even when I'm laughing
I am barely human.

RUTH AND REX HAVE A WAY

of wearing it all down, the crocodile transformed into something
more like an iguana, creeping along the branches of my thoughts
slow and jerky—

its jaws don't make me tremble in the same way; just make me feel
slow and jerky too. I'm out of practice talking to anyone but Leah
and Mandy.

I am stiff and rusty like the Tin Man, with a dash of the Lion:
no heart, no courage.

Too much brain.

EVEN WITH LETTUCE STUCK IN HER TEETH

Ruth is like a flame
that's almost bright enough to illuminate
the inky river down below,
which the three of us
stare at while we lean over the barricade.

I feel like a wolf in the woods,
drawn toward a campfire
and dreaming of becoming a dog.

This is such a weird town,
Ruth says, looking around.
All this river and no one here
to enjoy it.
Where is everybody?

Wildwood, I say.

Or bowling, adds Rex.
One of like thirty alleys.

Why so much bowling? Ruth asks,
and something about it is funny.

Ruth talks with what
my grandmother called "tone."
The kind of thing that a teacher could never
write on a detention slip
because the words themselves are nothing.

A creative tongue, I think, and immediately sink
into a blush that removes me from the conversation
because it sounded too much like sex
and I'm always thinking about sex
even when I don't want to.

Chicago, Ruth is saying when I tune back in.
Like actually Chicago. Not the suburbs.

Why would you move here? Rex says,
moving his tongue out and around

like it's pushing something bitter out.
It's the kind of thing I would never do
but Ruth laughs.

I'm just here for the summer.
My mom is a pediatrician and apparently y'all
have really good hospitals.

We do, Rex says confidently
and I just nod because I have no idea.

Whatever the reason, I'm just glad she's here.
She's the kind of girl who turns the air
to glitter. Like Leah, she seems to contain
something gold, and for a moment I feel

less like a crocodile
more like a magpie.

UP CLOSE, REX HAS EYES LIKE A TURTLE'S SHELL—

green-flecked brown, gold.
They just look hazel to me.

Ruth is the one who makes this comparison.

Her mother's brother had a terrarium, she tells us,
the size of a pool table. Turtles, some
the size of acorns, some like coffee cups,

roaming the lands carefully crafted
by her uncle's hands. Tiny fish too, all of them
in the universe of glass where houseplants
were rooted like shade trees.

It sounds beautiful, Rex says.

It was. It's the thing I miss most.

Well you can look in my eyes whenever you miss it, Rex says.

He's flirting, I realize
with some alarm. The magpie
of my heart takes a dip.

*Did I mention it stank
to high heaven?* Ruth adds.

Her tone, always laughing.
I can't tell if she's flirting or not—
maybe Rex can't either.

Lettuce, I say to her, pointing
at my own tooth, mirror
image. *Right there.*

She tongues it out.
It makes me swallow
my heart.

*You can't trust anyone who doesn't tell you
when you have something in your teeth,* she says.

Hey! Rex cries, laughing. *It's too dark!*

And full of terrors, Ruth says.
We're getting used to laughing
as a group—
even me.
It's dark and we have already escaped
one terror.

I think with Ruth here
glitter-gold
nothing evil would dare
come close, even if
it came incognito
with my face.

Maybe I can make myself
be okay. Or at the very least
 pretend.

RUTH DRIVES US HOME

and it turns out me and Rex live close, just a few short miles.
 I wonder if he takes the bus, if he left a car at Wildwood,
if he has a sibling who drives him places the way Mandy used to
 drive me.
 Maybe he doesn't have a car because he got a DUI.   (Why
would he have a DUI, Ariel?) I've never seen him in school so he
must go somewhere else, but if he lives close to me wouldn't he go
to my school?   Maybe he's homeschooled, maybe his parents
are religious fanatics.   (Why would they be religious fanatics,
 Ariel?)   Maybe when he got his DUI they got really into the

church.   (He didn't get a DUI, Ariel.)   I wonder what Ruth
will think when she finds out.   Will she ever be able to meet his
    parents?   If they're fanatics they're probably racist.   (Ariel, you
                    have no idea what his parents are like.)   What if

JUST ME AND RUTH

and when we get to my house
she turns off the car.

So I never got to say thank you
for getting me the job
at Wildwood. Why
did you do that?

I can't tell her it's because
I thought she was beautiful
or because the tips of her braids
are my favorite color
and it felt like a sign.

I don't want Leah in this car,
don't want to say *my best friend*
left, would you like to be
my new best friend?

All the calculations
that happen in my head are
too calculated
for anywhere outside it.

I don't know.
You seemed cool,

which isn't a lie
(even though I'm a good liar)
and she nods, accepting
this as truth but maybe
wishing I would say more.

I want to say more. I want to sit
here for an hour
and hear about Chicago
and terrariums
and if this is her car

but my head is full—
what if I start talking about serial killers?

Did you know locals believe
a serial killer has been operating
in Chicago for years, unapprehended?

That alone wouldn't be so bad
except the thoughts in my head
are like the root system
of a fragile plant.

Tug on one, and you see
they're all connected—pull
a thread and my disguise unravels,

clothes fall away to reveal
a tower of swarming insects.

Do you like working there? I ask.
It's the only normal question I can think of.

She leans over the steering wheel, stretching
like a cat. *Sort of. It seemed like a weird*
place to work. Like it would have a lot
of stories, you know?

I nod at that because, yes
Wildwood has lots of stories—
some of them are mine
and some of them are Leah's
and all of them are painted neon
with the colors of the fair

but after I say good night
and wave awkwardly at the silver
Volkswagen, I think about the stories
not yet written, and I want
Ruth
to be in them.

I'M NOT/NEVER READY TO GO HOME

The kitchen light is on, and I imagine my father
in there with his early-winter eyes, not quite cold
but somehow bare.

I watch Ruth's car disappear, then redirect my feet.

Three miles to Fine 5.

The dark theater swallows me up.
It's something called *Lolita*
and I'm so grossed out I switch showings
halfway through, slide into *Twister*.

The tornadoes make me think of Ruth
the way the wind fills up her car
the way it seems to power her forward.

What is my wind?
Most days the only thing that seems
to drive me forward
is the idea of staying one step ahead
of the croc in my stomach.

What kind of life is this—
afraid of myself
afraid of what I might do
afraid of what I've done and forgotten I did?

In the third row, there's a man with his hand
down his pants and at first I forget I'm not in *Lolita*—
the sick feeling has followed me into *Twister*.

There are six other people in the theater
and every now and then he checks
over his shoulder to make sure no one is looking
    or maybe to ensure that someone is.

I can't wait for the end to leave, step out into the summer night
wishing a cyclone would come and sweep the whole block away
peel us all up shingle by shingle and scatter us to the wind.

I WALK THE THREE MILES

and get home after midnight,
but before I do I have to trudge
through crowded lines outside bars
where white guys all with the same haircut
jostle in my path, then talk to each other
with volume meant for me:

Damn that bitch is tall, dude
I'd climb that beanstalk!
Are you sure that's not a man, dude?

It's not until I'm locking the front door
behind me that I find my comeback
in the mess of my thoughts:

Yes I'm sure I'm not a man
because if I was I wouldn't be trying
to hide the beast—
I'd be in a movie theater jacking off
or in the backseat of a car
with my hands around a girl's throat

I don't even know if that's true
and it doesn't make me feel better
knowing that all the things

that are wrong with me
all the thoughts I think
that are the wrong size
and too red
are yet another thing to add
to the list of abnormality:

that these thoughts are inside
the head
of a girl.

I'VE GOTTEN ALL THE MERMAID JOKES.

Everyone always wants to joke about Ariel:

Oh what a dumb bitch, the jokes go
traded her voice for a boyfriend
what a dummy—typical girl!

But anyone who watched the movie closely would know
that it wasn't Eric she wanted more than anything in the sea:

it was legs.

Ariel was so desperate to change a part of her body
into something that could take her
where she wanted to go, that she gave up something else

and I get it, Princess,
I really do

because I don't think there's anything I love as much
as you loved to sing, but I'd probably give up anything
to change my brain into something
that could carry me where I wanted to go.

Except, no offense, but at least
you had the whole ocean.

All I have
is swamp.

I CAN'T STAY IN BED.

Without my phone there is no
way to douse the thoughts.

How can I explain?

It's like my brain is on fire.

I throw my door open, anything
to clear the flames—roam
through the dark house
that still doesn't feel
like home.

But it's not dark.
The kitchen light is on
and my dad is at the sink,

his back to me, shoulders tense,
muttering under his breath.

Are you okay? I ask
and he jumps, jerks his head
around to look at me.

What are you doing up? he snaps.

(Mom wonders why
I never talk to him.)

But before I can even reply
his eyes sweep down,
taking in my bare legs.

Jesus, Ariel, put
some clothes on.

Then he's back to scrubbing
whatever is in the sink—
the water so hot steam
rises. It must be scalding
his hands.

And in my head, the whisper:
He sees exactly what you are.
He cannot bear to look.

I'VE ONLY EVER HAD ONE BOYFRIEND—

in sixth grade, when everyone was getting boyfriends.
I knew what it meant to be gay because Mandy
has always told me everything, has always
been my sisterly encyclopedia
translating the world into terms
I can understand. But for some reason

when I was 11 I thought being gay
was something someone else told you
you were, an assignment you received
on your birthday or something—
a letter in the mail.

I thought that the reason watching
Maxie Morrison put her hair into a ponytail
was as interesting to me as watching an HBO limited series
was because she was cool and pretty
and I should learn how to be those things
as well, by watching.

    (Nope—lesbian
    actually.)

But before that, I wore the shoes that were expected
to fit, and that meant telling Brent Worley
that yes I would be his girlfriend
and feeling a queasy quagmire
swirling in my stomach whenever
he would text me. Three years older

and he had already kissed several
girls and had sex too and he always
wanted to talk about it and tell me
all the things he would do "when
I let him."

Six weeks later he broke up with me
because his family joined a new church
and he said he couldn't
have a girlfriend who thought
about premarital sex

and even though I never really liked him
I spent weeks after the breakup
scrolling through my texts, studying
my replies, trying to see what I said
that made him think I wanted
any of the things he had been
so interested in.

The next time I saw him was at an art fair
my mom helped organize, and he was wearing
a shirt and tie with a golden cross pin
and he wouldn't look me
in the eye.

"NO ONE CAN MAKE YOU FEEL INFERIOR WITHOUT YOUR CONSENT"

was the poster on the back of Mrs. Warren's door
all last year and sometimes I would stare at it
wondering if Mrs. Warren was the one who tacked it
up there. After all, Mrs. Warren is the one
who sent Gabby Phillips to in-school suspension
for wearing a skirt two inches shorter than dress code.

Maybe the poster has an asterisk I can't see
from my desk:

No one* can make you feel inferior without your consent
    *unless that person is me.

Either way, I try to believe the quote,
but I wonder if Mrs. Warren (or Eleanor
Roosevelt) really knows what
we're up against—

it's like plugging the holes of a sinking
ship with our fingers
and Jesus, Eleanor, I only have
ten
and I need my toes too
if I'm going to count all the things
that are leaking into this boat
of my head.

Everything else aside, it's been six years
since Brent was my "boyfriend"

and I still sometimes think
of how he made me feel

like a slug.

Like I'm making my way through life
hideous without meaning to be—
like behind me there is a trail that I can't see
but when the sun shines
just right
illuminates the slime I leave behind.

Sometimes (more than sometimes)
it makes me pause—
reviewing everything I say and do
like checking security footage
waiting for the light to shift
and all the filth that I exude
to become crystal clear.

BACK IN THE CAVE OF MY ROOM

I look down
at my own legs
and notice
how pale they are

how my knees are reddish
and my feet blue.
Cold blood, I think, even
as I can hear Mandy say
Too much sitting.

Cold blood. Like the reptile
inside me is transforming my body.
I still don't know   for sure

if I stabbed Jason with a dart.
My feet seem wrong, I decide,
and so do my knees.

How do I control my blood?
How can anything beneath the skin
be mastered?

I walk in circles around my room
Walking is good
for circulation, I think.
I can make my blood warm.

I haven't done this for a while—
I tried to stop
but it only lasts for so long.

These circles are good. I count them

9
   10
      20
         30

I stop at 60.
When I look at my feet they're not blue

anymore and I think *good, poor circulation
can kill you.*

So many things can kill you.
Not always a man (or girl) with a knife.

It's 4:34am and I wonder
if my father is afraid of me,
if the sight of my cold blue feet
blinks like an alarm in his eyes,
if he knows what it all means.

I do four more circles, 64 because
it's divisible by 4 exactly 16 times,
which is also divisible by 4.

It seems good. My heart is beating
a little more quickly, I feel warm.

A thought arrives: *This is how I keep my dad safe
from me.* The thought hisses a little
on the *s,* and I wonder if the crocodile
has learned to speak. But either way I know.

These blood-warming circles
will keep that look from crossing his face
will keep the fear out of his head.

I hope he can sleep tonight.

With the circles done and my feet no longer blue
I slither into bed
and eventually I'm unconscious.

Everyone is safe.

EXCEPT FELICIA PALMER
She's
already
gone.

WHEN I GET TO WILDWOOD IN THE MORNING
Mr. Malcolm catches me as I slip through
the employee gate, sweating from walking
six miles.

Megga wants to see you, he says
and something about the way he looks
down over his glasses tells me I might be
in trouble, that he knows something
I don't know. Mr. Malcolm is mostly the king
of minding his business, so he keeps walking,
whistling and jingling his keys.

Usually Jason is with him but today
he is not.

REUNITED WITH MY PHONE

I have a couple texts Mandy sent at midnight
I can only guess at some of the letters
through the cracks in my screen:
Mandy: no good night text?
Mandy: are you asleep?
Mandy: I hope you're okay

I AM SEVENTEEN YEARS OLD

and my sister has to send me a bedtime
text to make sure I'm not falling apart.

I wonder if she texted my parents too
to make sure they're alive
to make sure I hadn't done anything to them
to make sure the crocodile didn't unzip
    itself from my flesh
      to roam the house.

She doesn't know that even without my phone
I found a way to keep everyone safe.

But as I make my way across Wildwood
the guilt swims through me like sharp-
finned fish. When Mandy got to college
I heard the way her voice got lighter
the way the deadweight of our parents'
house fell away like cut hair.

I am the only anchor holding her ship
back from the wild, wonderful places
the wind wants to carry it. I have to
cut this rope, I have to
free her sails.

When I text her back, I keep it short
because the cracks in my phone's screen
distort all the words
distort all the thoughts
    make them look jagged and torn
    and in a way
    that's exactly as it should be.

TEXT TO MANDY

Everything is fine. I was hanging with friends last night and broke
my phone. I'm feeling much better lately, so don't worry, okay?
Everything is fine.

IN THE PIT OF MY STOMACH

the crocodile turns over
and sighs,
content.

THE LOCO LOCOMOTIVE IS THE SCARIEST RIDE IN THE PARK

to the people who ride it—that is,
children under 42" tall.
It's their favorite ride—mine, too.

Blue engine, three cars,
red caboose—entry-level
roller coaster for future
speed demons cramming
into line with sticky hands.

I love little kids, love the idea
of this being something
just for them, conquering
tiny fears, then choosing
to get back in line again
and again.

They smell like sunscreen
and bug spray and French fries,
they scream like train whistles
when I switch the lever
that sends the machine rolling
forward on the track.

I was trained on Loco Loco
my first summer here—a 90-second ride,
three curves, one tunnel, one hump,

and back around. The only thing
is that it's as old as Mr. Malcolm

and every now and then I worry
about it going from the Little Engine
That Could go up the hill to
the Little Engine That Could
fly into outer space.

But

hot sun. Free soda. The music
like tin and rhinestone, the air
melting like taffy on pavement.
Kids laughing, the train squeaking,
and me smiling.

CARNIVAL TIME

the rhythm of the day
rolls in the loops of train music
five songs that repeat and repeat
30 minutes for all five tunes—
this is how I keep track
of how long I've been here.

The sun beats down
I sip Sprite

I get no text messages

I think of my first
summer here

laughing with Leah, head empty
of ugly thoughts

She always said *you worry
too much*

How could she have known
what I would become

how could she have known
that the thing

I was so worried about
would eventually

turn out to be me?

IT'S FIVE MINUTES UNTIL THE END OF MY SHIFT WHEN IT HAPPENS:

the Loco Loco
reaching the end
of its loop
and instead of resting,
chugging on

    instead of pausing,
    the wheels grow hot

and hotter, screaming
as loud as the oblivious
kids in the cars and caboose
    screaming screaming screaming

      the whole bright machine
      colliding with empty space
      blood and steel and tiny bones
      parents in silent horror
      as their children careen into the sky
      then down to the ground

        and me in the metal booth
        hand on the lever
        urging it all into motion.

I HAVE A LICENSE BUT I DON'T DRIVE

for the same reason I no longer take the bus—

one more thing the crocodile   my silent radio host

has cut me off from.
It doesn't matter that I was good

at parallel parking, or that I always
drove the speed limit.

The technicalities don't matter.

What matters:
    every time I drove on the highway, the emcee would ask me
    over and over

        what would happen if you closed your eyes?
        what would happen if you closed your eyes?
        what would happen if you closed your eyes?

and sometimes I did
    long blink

and sometimes I can still feel the car drift
my whole body
the whole universe inside my head
    drift

and in those brief moments
the moment where I don't fight—
    the burst of relief
like crushing a grape in my teeth.

Every second of every day
a fight against a beast I can't see
except when I look
in my own eyes.

I don't drive anymore.

It's not worth
the risk.

THREE TRAILERS MAKE A TRIANGLE

behind Megga's, and inside them is the gravel pit
and picnic tables—the break area
for Wildwood employees,
cemetery for a billion cigarette butts.

I know what I have to do:
I use the pit to walk 64 circles and repeat
what used to be my bedtime prayer
but now feels necessary during the day

> *I'm okay she's okay they're okay.*
> *I'm okay she's okay they're okay.*
> *I'm okay she's okay they're okay.*

I repeat it until the circles run out
and by then the pressure in my chest
feels like it has shrunk enough
that my ribs don't feel cracked.

Everyone is safe.

I didn't think you smoked.

I didn't hear Rex until he was beside me
feet crunching on gravel.

We lock eyes, and he sees something
in mine, because he squints.

Long pause.

Ruth clocks out in five minutes—
want to hang?

BUT WHAT IF

I transform
What if a knife appears
in the backseat
of Ruth's car
and I cut both of their
throats?

I HAVE A MEMORY THAT STAYS WITH ME

Mandy beside me with a candy cane
poking out from between her lips like a tusk,
her hair blowing wild in highway wind.

My father is driving us
somewhere
there are lunch boxes at our feet
my legs are long enough so that my toes
can only just brush against the smile
of SpongeBob.

We're slowing down, exit ramp

red light
when my father's eyes find us
in the rearview mirror.
He doesn't talk to us much
now or then—
he is grim and distant.
Work, our mother always guesses.

When he sees my sister's peppermint tusk
he doesn't smile. He drives on.
It is only when she is climbing
out of the car that he says

You could choke.

WAITING ON THE HOOD OF RUTH'S CAR

while Rex is in the bathroom. It feels strange
to be alone. Crocodile doing flip-flops
begging for attention.

What if you open your mouth to speak
and something else comes out instead?
word vomit or literal vomit,
or all the soft thoughts you have?
What if you start to speak and you grab instead?

Sometimes I think

Drugs

Drugs could help
Drugs like zoo plexiglass smudged with fingerprints
between me and the reptile of my brain

Ooh Daddy look at the teeth

Don't worry baby they can't hurt you in there

Drugs like a rope to the bottom of a well
stuffing myself in the bucket and hauling
myself out of a dark hole.

Ariel? Are you listening?

    Sorry got distracted. Tell me again.

*I was just talking about this script I'm working on. You wanna be in
a movie?*

    Sure.

You'd probably be a great actor.

    Why?

Call it a hunch.

RUTH'S CAR IS NOT RUTH'S CAR

It's a rental, she says when Rex asks.

Her mother spoils her with money
instead of time—she only has the former.

She insists on me coming down for the summer
like we'll actually see each other.
You know she doesn't even know
I have this job?

Ruth laughs as she drives us around
the city that we know
and she doesn't.

I guess she thought I would just sit at home
all day? I could drive back up to Chicago
and back before she even got off a shift.

She pats the dash of the Volkswagen
she has named Tempera,
co-conspirators.

Whenever she turns the wheel
her fingernails flash—
long daggers, pastel pink. With my eyes blurred
she is a Monet: all the colors
of water lilies, stream of dawn.
She's too soft for the neon of Wildwood.

I still don't know why you wanted to work there,
I say from the backseat. When Rex offered me
the front, I refused. It's bad enough
that I'm in this car at all.

The stories, Ariel, the stories,
Ruth says, slaps the steering wheel
for emphasis.

This whole city has those, Rex says.
Shit, I could tell you some.

SO HE DOES.

The purple comb in Ruth's cup holder becomes a microphone,
Rex a tour guide, rolling his voice as we roll around corners.

On your left you'll see the Speedway that someone pretended to rob
with an aluminum foil gun for a TikTok and ended up in prison

Up here on your right is the twelfth bowling alley in three square miles.
It is, as you can see, totally packed.

For the moment, passengers, you can rest your eyes and take a nap,
as for the next twenty blocks there is nothing but a parade of strip
malls that contain dollar stores, restaurants, and laundromats,
one of which was the setting for a music video but no one remembers
which one.

Oh, and here is one of the malls that shut down. And ah, yes, here is another one of the malls that shut down. Here is one of the malls that shut down but that they reopened as an indoor driving range. It is, as you can see, totally packed.

Ah, now one of our famed medical complexes. Got cancer? You've come to the right place. Got a rare autoimmune disorder? You've arrived! Want to begin hormone replacement therapy? Come on in! But only if your parents aren't gender essentialist assholes with bills their conservative parents still pay and therefore send you to single-sex boarding school so no one has to look at you except for on holidays when everyone is already drunk and arguing.

Welcome home! Can't wait to leave, can you?

Relatable.

Oh, and there is Karate Kev's, one of the only establishments that rivals bowling alleys in number of locations. If you want to learn martial arts from a white guy who got so rich from his classes that they put his face on a building downtown, look no further!

And I say, *That's my dad.*

"THAT'S MY DAD."

At first Rex only tilts his head, like maybe I was talking to myself. But then Ruth's eyes are in the rearview, brows low, wondering if I'm trying to be funny like Rex. Rex is used to being funny—I am not. So when he turns to look into the backseat, he's still smiling.

You're lying, he says, half laugh.

Kevin Burns. Married Melody Wickham, now Melody Burns.
Two children. Ariel Burns and Miranda Burns. Cat—Barbie Burns.

He stares, Ruth's eyes widening, sparkling with a laugh.

You're serious, Rex says.

I lift my hand and silently, gently karate-chop the air.

MY DAD HAS DONE KARATE FOR AS LONG AS I CAN REMEMBER.

I'm seventeen and I think I can remember when he got his black belt, another somber white man presenting it like a folded mamba across arms straight and stiff.

For a while, Mandy did it too—classes and tournaments. I know where the box of dusty trophies is, pushed all the way under her bed with folded-up gis, yellowed at the armpits. She learned the hard way:

Karate was the only way you could get Dad to see you.

But only if you did it just right.

Mandy was uncoordinated but in a furious way. Every step was an elephant's, every swing was its trunk. Heavy and purposeful but never quite right. *You have to be light,* our father would say. *You have to feel your energy moving you across the floor.*

I didn't bother. Younger sister, watchful child, I watched her flicker into visibility when she stood in his ranks at the dojo before it was his dojo.

Then I watched her flicker out.

"YOUR DAD IS KARATE KEV?!"

Ruth doesn't have the history of our town to understand why Rex is cackling in the front seat. He leans against the window he's laughing so hard.

Oh my god, I'm sorry, he says. *I'm sorry.*

> *Don't be.* I *don't have to be embarrassed just because he's embarrassing.*

Ooh nice, Ruth says, like she's dog-earing a page in a book. She believes me. She believes that I'm not embarrassed and all I can think about myself is *Ariel, you lie about everything.*

I'm sorry, Rex repeats, snorting.

> *I mean, me too,* I reply. A little closer to the truth.

Someone fill me in, Ruth says. She has pulled into the Karate Kev's parking lot.

I'd love to, Rex says, and we're already laughing. *This white guy— ARIEL'S DAD—started a karate dojo and other white people liked it so much that they turned him into a local celebrity. Now every time there's a community event or something, Karate Kev—WHO IS ARIEL'S FATHER—has a tent there, giving away ninja key chains and free first classes. Sometimes they have him on for the lottery to draw the winner—*

That's not him, I interrupt. *That's Greg. My dad is actually shy. He'd never do that. Greg, though . . .*

Greg likes the limelight, Ruth says, nodding at the big glass windows. Stories. Character.

Inside, two rows of mostly white teenagers stand in horse stance while Sensei Whoever barks from the front of the room. I know how the air feels just by looking—hot and close. Sweat and cedar.

What if I went inside with a sledgehammer and smashed every single mirror, glass coating the floor like pixie dust, everyone's feet bleeding and someone shouting *That's Sensei Kevin's daughter, that's her,* and then I'd have to use the sledgehammer on their heads because—

So do you do it too?

I turn down the volume of the crocodile and find Rex and Ruth turned around in their seats, looking at me.

Do what?

Karate.

I am suddenly very glad that I never put on the stiff white uniform, never yanked a belt of any color at my waist. I can feel their expectations—they're already half sure. I have to lie about a lot of things but not this.

Fuck that.

When Ruth explodes in laughter, a tiny drop of spit launches from her mouth and lands on the cracked screen of my phone, cradled in my lap.

We all look down at it, that single speck of saliva.

Then we all explode, laughing so loud it feels like the windshield should shatter, but it doesn't.

RUTH LIKES TO DRIVE.

She likes our highways, how big and empty
she says they are.
Your lake is tiny compared to Lake Michigan, she says,
but it's still good driving scenery.

She wedges her braids behind her back
and then opens all the windows
as she glides up the on-ramp.

No music—
It's overstimulating.
She doesn't like to talk

while we're all going 75
going nowhere.

I don't feel as bad cuz it's electric,
she says. *Do you ever feel
like everything you do matters
too much and also not at all?*

Rex nods because he always nods
but that doesn't mean it's not real.

What do you want to be, I say
when we're off the highway
and the wind isn't so loud

I want to be a cop, she says

and, never mind, Rex doesn't *always* nod—
at this, he jerks his head sideways before

Ruth cackles and screams SIKE
into the night's blue breeze.

RUTH WANTS TO BE AN ACTRESS

and also a screenwriter:
The world is a stage, she says.

*How else are we supposed to make it through
stuck in this body, stuck in this life?*

Who can possibly make it through
without pretending to be somebody else?

How else can we get to the end of this race
without walking in somebody else's shoes?

"STORIES," I SAY

and Ruth catches my eye in the mirror,
her glint of approval, of acknowledgment
that I have not only heard but held her truths.

Stories, she echoes. *An actress is a storyteller—*
maybe I want to write the script too.
Do it all.
Make it mine.

Do you ever feel like there's a show someone cast you in
but you never auditioned and there aren't enough
        costumes?

I don't answer, but in the lonely
backseat, I nod yes. Yes.

ENVY

I watch the back of Rex's head, feeling
envious. Mandy asked me once if I thought
I was trans.

I don't think so. How would I know?

Do you ever feel like you're a boy?

I don't think so. What does a boy feel like?

I think if you know, you know.

Do you feel like a girl?

Yes. Do you?

I guess so. What does a girl feel like?

I don't know. It's just . . . me.

Car or carnival
sometimes it feels
like everyone around me
knows something I don't—

that there was a blueprint
of their identity they received
at birth, and build

the architecture of their life
brick by solid brick
while I am using
Legos.

"HOW DO YOU KNOW YOU'RE A GIRL?"

Sometimes my brain spits out questions
like the launcher at a batting cage.
Usually it's just for me to swing at
but today I'm in the cage
with Ruth.

> *What makes you feel*
> *like a girl?*

She feels me looking at her, and her eyes find mine
in the rearview mirror. We're going fast and usually
that's when she's quiet but we've been talking about
    stories—
she's in an answering place.

I don't think it's about how I feel
it's about what I do
    and I do
what I like.

I am soft and bossy
and I want hair to my ass
and nails like leopard claws
and sneakers and messy food
    I
    am messy food
I am impulse and dark-night logic
I am North Star, Capricorn, and chicken bones
I am thick legs and flat chest

I am whatever the fuck
I call myself.

The world is a stage,
remember?
I am what I
perform
enough times
to know it
by heart.

Then we're driving silently again,
my brain and heart humming
and the night is black and the stars are bright
and Ruth is one of them.

SAYING GOOD NIGHT FEELS LIKE THE END OF DANCING—

I am reluctant to leave the car, where conversation bubbles like
ginger ale, making most of my ugly thoughts light and floaty, far
away. But as after a night of dancing, I feel an ache, like the need to
slip off my shoes before my ankles give way.

The house is quiet and charcoal-dark. I imagine Mandy in her
dorm, maybe studying, maybe kissing.

In ~~our~~ my room, I feel the hot swell, simmering shadows that have
been lurking in my head since I turned the key of the Loco Loco.

The crash of metal, the screech of
brakes and children, smoke rising from the
wreckage, and me watching from the booth,
Lake Placid, crocodile in the still waters.
Could I even pretend it was an accident?

Stop, Ariel. Elephant ears.
Bowling alleys.

The toe of my shoe nudging a corpse

Sketch pad. How do you make a face?
How can I create anything
besides the visions my brain
feeds me like raw meat?

Dead children trapped under hot metal,
torn and smoking, blood leaking out like
from a butcher block

I put pencil to paper, try to create
something not from a nightmare.
I try I try I try
but my crocodile knows
when it's being tricked—
it won't be distracted.

Parents reaching for the bodies of their
children, the sound of them wailing
mixing with the carnival tunes

Enough. I google symptoms,
research all the signs:
how to spot a serial killer

I want to be able to spot   myself:
I want to send these lists of facts
to my sister, ask her to read
every one, then ask: do you see me?
Do you see me? Please say
no.

It's not working. The answers
are there as they always are
but it's not enough. Talking
to Rex and Ruth about my father
has stirred up something
that can't be shifted:
when I look for reassurance
from the libraries of criminal minds
all I see is *strained relationship*
with parents; early childhood violence
and fantasies of hurting others.

When I close my eyes I can see my father
and the distance in his gaze—
never wanting to get too close.

He has always looked at me and been afraid
of what he sees.

Did he look at my baby teeth
and see fangs?
Has he always
                known?

MY PHONE INTERRUPTS MY 120TH CIRCLE

Ruth: hey creeps

Rex: I'm going to save this text for when you're a famous actress so I can say SHE ONCE TEXTED ME "hey creep"

Ruth: I'll dedicate my first Oscar to yall

Rex: But what if I directed the movie.

Ruth: Oh? You want to be a director?

Rex: I've done a couple things.

Ruth: Oh??

Rex: just little projects so far

Ruth: okay Taika!

Rex: Ariel, do you have any secret ambitions we should know about?

Ruth: Ariellllll

Ruth: Ariellllllllllll

Ariel: hi

Rex: there she is!

Ruth: Join us in Hollywood?

Ariel: I don't think I'm qualified

Rex: set design, perhaps. Wardrobe. You're an artist!

Ariel: eh

Ruth: don't act like we don't know—we see you, Ariel!

MY PHONE FEELS HOT IN MY HANDS

like the thing that usually cools the coals has turned into holy water against a devil's skin.

I am curled on my bed when the crocodile nudges me—hard.

More circles.

Truth descends from the ceiling—a murder of crows alighting on each shoulder. I know for sure: I have passed the point of curiosity, of wondering. Today the lever of the Loco Loco was gripped in my sweating hand. I could envision the effort—next to nothing—to urge that lever into action. The knowledge had churned down my arm and set my fingers tingly. I could've done it so easily.

The time for wondering has passed. If there is anything human in me—I can feel parts of my brain that are free of scales—then it's that which tells me what to do now.

Prevention.

Circles.

I release my knees and look at my feet: bluish in the lamplight. Leap out of bed.

64.

Then 64 more, because it wasn't just my hand on the train, but thinking about it in Ruth's car.

Then 64 more, because every circle keeps me from being the thing she sees glinting in wet pavement.

Then 64 more, because also in Ruth's car I watched her smiling in the mirror and imagined pressing my lips against hers, my hands around her waist.

It all feels related. If my hands are capable of crashing a train, they are capable of anything.

My hands wrapped around her throat.

64 more.

When I'm finished, it's 3am and my feet are not blue. I have walked the crocodile out. Sleep pulls me down into its thick swamp and finally my head is empty.

Everyone is safe.

SOCIAL MEDIA CAN BE A RABBIT HOLE

but rabbits are safe in their holes, aren't they?
That's how it feels: burrowing
into information that (as long as it carefully
avoids certain subjects) feels like a deep warm
hole in the earth while winter rages
cold and white overhead.

In that hole I find threads of worlds
I would never have seen,
peepholes into lives lived that always
feel completely different from mine—

until inevitably they become the same.

On Reddit I find a thread of animators
    (I have thought it would be cool to be an animator)

talking about different projects they've worked on—
all anonymous so they're allowed to share the details:

I animated this show once and a guy got fired
for trying to sneak in seashells that looked like dicks
all along the beach scenes

I worked on this one movie and we had to fight
them to let us put muscles on the girl
character who is superstrong . . .
but, like, she's superstrong! She can lift a cow!
She needs muscles! They wanted her narrow-
waisted and willow-armed.
It didn't even make sense!

Why was She-Hulk
like a size 6?

Girls can be anything, they say,
as long as they still fit into that box.

How can she lift the cow without muscles,
man? Tell me!
Even magic
is grounded in reality!

THOUGHTS ABOUT MAGIC

I've always believed in it. My earliest
memories are wrapped up in spells:
imagining I could talk

to animals, believing with all
my heart that if I just
concentrated
hard enough, I could make
the door close without lifting a finger.

Coincidence felt like magic.

If she wears pink on Thursday
then that means she likes me back.

I've always been looking for a way out of reality.
I've always tried to look at everything
expected of me and magic myself
into fitting.

Conclusion is obvious:
if I were Cinderella
I would have never

made it to the ball.

SWEAT IS ONE THING THAT HAS ALWAYS MADE ME FEEL HUMAN

Mr. Cipinko gave out school-branded cloths to all of us
who came to weight lifting regularly, square and maroon
and marked in the corner with a Trojan helmet in gold.
It was the right kind of material, soaking up sweat
instead of sliding it around.

Drop your rear, he'd say.
He was never weird
about referring to my butt
or anyone else's.

A body was a body—
muscle suit
flesh and blood and bone.

There is a difference between meat and meat:
there's the kind that someone's teeth
want to rip
and there's the kind that we all are.

Sweat and blood and exhaustion feel good
in this body.

It means it's working
It means I'm doing something right.

Strong and stronger
only in one box
labeled

Useful.

TEXTS WITH MANDY IN THE MORNING

Mandy: Hey are you okay?
Ariel: I'm fine. Are you okay?

Mandy: I didn't hear from you much yesterday.

Ariel: My phone's broken—hard to text

Mandy: What happened?

Ariel: Dropped it.

Mandy: If you need another phone, my old one is in my drawer

Ariel: cool thx

Mandy: How are mom and dad?

Ariel: alive

Mandy: not what I meant. I just haven't talked to them either.

Ariel: just busy. Mom joined neighborhood association.

Mandy: of course she did. Some things never change

Ariel: sure they do. They get worse

I KNOW THE WORD *GENTRIFICATION*

It looks different up close.

When I get out of bed, the machines
outside have already begun their work
and through the window
my mother stands on the corner
in the newness of the day

chatting with two more people
who are poised like sentinels
as old becomes new,
as what was flattens
under what will be.

Everyone has a dream
of being safe and good.

No one wants to think
they're doing any harm.

Everyone thinks
they're an exception.

No drop of water thinks
it's part of a tidal wave.

MY SISTER'S BEDSIDE TABLE

is as organized as it's always been. The invisible line down the
center of the room we share/d, her things stacked and squared and
unwrinkled on one side; on the other, the spill of my notebooks,
surges of loose paper and dead pens.

There isn't much left in her nightstand, everything carried away to
college. The day she finished packing I sat cross-legged on my bed
watching, knowing she wasn't coming back. Rat in maze chews
through screen. Fox chews leg clean off. Patient Mandy, channeling
all her energy into her exit plan while I scribbled sad/mad poems.

I never saw her keep a diary,
so I'm surprised when I find one in the drawer.

Tucked at the back, not so much a diary as pages of reminders,
observations, and lots and lots of lists, organized by bullet points,
color coded, as aesthetically pleasing as her side of the room.

Had I opened this notebook and found confessions, I would have
closed it. Mandy doesn't believe that boundaries between countries

are real, or even that they need to exist, but that boundaries
between people must, and I agree. She has always made such sense.
She isn't a fox with a chewed foot, no. She is a rat of NIMH. Bided
her time and made her way.

And me behind her, struggling. Straight-A Mandy, cool clean
Mandy, smaller and smarter than me. Me, big little-sister who likes
to read but can never remember what was on the pages.

I know my sister well. I am not surprised by the form this diary
takes. Lists for everything:

- College pros and cons
- Potential internships
- Documentaries and movies
- Words she likes the sound of + their etymology
- Cities around the world with the best rock formations
- Companies with ethical fabric sourcing
- Dog breeds that were overbred as the result of pop cultural moments
- College application essay ideas
    - (And that's where I see my name)

"COLLEGE ESSAY IDEAS"

- Resistance to therapy in Christian communities
- Parents who don't believe in therapy
- The pros and cons of Christian-only schools
- Ariel

WELL, SHIT.

A moment ago
I believed in boundaries.

Now I am turning them
into dust.

It's easy to find
my sister's phone.

She gave me permission,
I think as I power
it on.

Not for this,
I answer
but that voice
is quiet.

It has too much
competition.

THE CROCODILE GOT MANDY INTO COLLEGE.

Drive → CollegeAppEssay-final.doc

In which Miranda Burns explains that her sister, Ariel Burns, is
the reason

she believes minors should be allowed to go to therapy without
parental consent
she believes prayer isn't a sufficient alternative to therapy
she was driven to apply to college to study religion

I drove Mandy to college.

I am a speeding bus, carrying her to Michigan
I am a speeding bus, roaring at her heels

It's a good essay. I don't have
to read it all to know
it is poignant
organized
rational—

all the things
that Mandy is.

Good daughter.

Phone, notebook
everything put away.

Me and my cracked screen
walking circles
into the rug.

I REMEMBER CHURCH

The kind of memory that feels like it might belong to someone else
because it's far and fuzzy.
Crimson carpet, mahogany pews. The smell of candle smoke, the
minister on the dais at the front, full of reminders and wisdom, anecdotes
that he tied to the hearts and futures of everyone in the congregation.

Turn to your neighbor and tell them they're blessed.

Turn to your neighbor and tell them you're blessed.

Then close your eyes with me and pray.

Keeping my eyes open felt like a childhood game back then, before
I knew better.

Eyes on the ceiling, eyes on the crystal light fixtures, tracing their
path to the floor and counting the heads of who would be killed if
the chandeliers fell.

Then eyes on my father, who always knew, with his forehead
pressed to his praying hands, lips moving fast, eyes shut so tight
that they were fists. Praying so hard that when we all opened our
eyes and said *amen,* the shape of his knuckle,

   red on his forehead.

Mandy was always beside me, and I thought she thought I was okay.

Turns out, she's seen the Devil in me all along.

PERFORMANCE

I think I know what Ruth meant about performance—
when I am honest (and I rarely am) I look at myself
and put an Oscar statue in my hands.

If my life is a call sheet, I audition for various characters:

Scene: Church
Character: Pious Daughter

Scene: School
Character: Studious Girl

Scene: Cafeteria
Character: Kind Friend

Scene: Carnival
Character: Good Employee

I don't think I asked Ruth the right question—
not *how do you know you're a girl?*
but *how do you know you're doing* girl *right?*

I can pretend to be so many things
but the longer I live the more I see

that *girl* and *good* are meant to be synonyms
and I'm not sure where that leaves
me.

WHENEVER I'M GETTING DRESSED

I do it as quickly as possible and away
from the mirror. I don't know when
I learned to hate my body or who taught me
but I do know there are days—moments—
when what I've learned lapses like summer:

out of the classroom
algebra pouring out
of my ear and into finally
green grass.

In those moments I feel free
in the same way that summer feels free:
eyes and expectations bricked up inside the school

and me big as a mountain and light as a feather,
looking in the mirror and liking what I see.

Today is not
one of those days.

This is not
one of those moments.

THE ONLY THING THAT COULD MAKE THIS MORNING WORSE IS MY PARENTS

and they do, they always do.
I find them in the kitchen:

> Mom—green smoothie, Lululemon pants and jacket

> Dad—sweat suit with Karate Kev's logo small on the chest, drinking tea

You need a better bra, Mom says when she sees me, frowning.
You're all flattened out.

My father says nothing, doesn't even look my way.
    He's barely here.
    He's barely here
            because I am here.

I have driven him to the far-off iceberg
where he has made his home.

I have driven Mandy
to Michigan.
I look at the sharp angles
of my mother's body
and realize I may have
driven her
here too.

"HOW IS LEAH?"

my mother asks, because she loves Leah—
the one thing we have in common.

She's in DC.

This is how it is: throw scraps,
enough to satisfy the question
without having to explain everything.

Leah was always the right kind of friend
for my mother: pretty and petite
and smiley, always with a boyfriend.

If she didn't have so many boyfriends
I would think twice before letting her
spend the night, my mom joked sometimes,
before she knew I was gay, when she was still
testing the ground, jokes like canaries
in the coal mine. Leah, my passport

to okay, my ticket to non-suspicion.
Between her and Mandy, I am the odd
sandwich: put me between enough
wholesome bread and you'll never notice
the meat is rotten.

"CAN YOU BRING UP THE GROCERIES BEFORE YOU LEAVE?"

my mother asks, because the delivery person left them
at the bottom of the stairs. *So lazy,* my mother sighs.

18 steps straight up—I almost say *Maybe if you tipped.*

But I can carry them all, bags looped over my forearms.
I climb the staircase step by step, slow
and steady. It feels like carrying a boulder up a mountain.

Strong enough to move a body
Strong enough to carry a corpse to the river
Strong enough to transport cinder blocks as anchors
Strong enough to pick up the whole thing,
body and bricks
and throw it in the water.

Wow, look at you, Mom says, uncomfortable.
Mountain
daughter. Mammoth
daughter.

Behemoth.

I am not just everything she is not—
I am everything she runs from being.
I am her face in water
rippled into monster.

I am not an infection
I am a tumor

I am a thing pushing against fragile skin
I am something waiting to be excised.

"WHAT HAPPENED TO YOUR FOOT?"

I'm always a little surprised by my dad
when he speaks without being spoken to—

even my mom seems taken aback,
pauses with green-smoothie froth on her lip.

He's looking at my bare feet—it's not
until he points that I notice the blood
down the back of one foot.

> **You did it you killed someone in your sleep**
> **went next door cut the neighbor's throat**
> **sliced her Pomeranian into pieces**
> **walked back up your stairs in a haze**
> **back to bed, sheets streaked with red...**

Lord, Ariel, what shoes have you been wearing?
Don't you have anything that won't
cut you to ribbons?

She's right—it's a bloody crescent
around the back of each heel
rubbed raw from 12ish miles every day in too-small shoes

The right foot is especially bad: the whole
area as tender and pink as a pork chop,
dried blood smeared around like spray paint.

After all the walking and the circles,
last night I felt outside my body—fuzzy and distant
only looking at my feet to make sure
they weren't blue.

Have you been going out? My mother says, sharp, sets the smoothie
down.
Wearing heels?

And be even taller?

It's from walking to work, I say quickly.

Walking? To Wildwood? What about the bus?

I spoke too fast. Thought too slow.

It just doesn't come sometimes. Weak. But no one cares.

You could be working right here in the neighborhood, my mother says.
All these new restaurants are hiring.

I could. Leah's brother does, always bragging
about the tips. But Leah's brother
is dark-eyed and symmetrical: handsome
bones like a sculpture made by someone
who loves him.

Too much talking as a waiter. Too much
smiling and banter.

Too many knives.
Too much attention to detail.
Too many eyes, too close.

At the very least drive the car
we bought you,
my father says. Eyes out the window
but voice bumpy with judgment.

At Wildwood we are responsible for one thing at a time.
Lift the bar, flip the lever, take the ticket.
I don't know how anyone
manages more.

Stop wearing shoes that are too small, my mother says,
puts her smoothie glass in the sink. My father
washes it quickly, steam rising, still gazing out the window.

Okay.

I WEAR A SIZE 12

but that number is unacceptable—
it's like trying to swallow a melon.

At the door to our house, my mother's
shoes are beside mine: little 7.5s
short and neat beside the expanse of the too-small 11s

I bought them knowing they were too small—
in the store, the diagonal mirrors angled
toward my feet made them stretch
and expand to clown proportions.

I knew that if the 11s looked like this
the 12s would be impossible.

I am too many things, all of them
too.

Too big
Too quiet
Too broad
Too off

I pass my reflection
on the way out the door
and the shape of me
takes up the entire mirror.

Sometimes I want to disappear
and that seems as impossible
as making the crocodile
turn to dust—
there's simply too much
     of me.

BEFORE MY GRANDMOTHER DIED, SHE CALLED ME A LATE BLOOMER.

She was always taken aback
by my squareness
    tallness
    my sharp edges

I think she was waiting for my breasts
up until her last breath: *You'll soften up, Ariel,*
you'll grow into yourself. I was only fourteen
when she passed but I wish I could have asked her
if she was wishing for me or for herself,
if she thought she was doing me a favor
by mourning the rectangle of my body.

This is the problem with sympathy:
you may show up to a funeral
with roses and a long skirt only
to find the widow in cutoffs, dancing
like a woodland fairy.

There's a cookie mold we're all
supposed to be, and not just that—
    that we're all supposed to *want.*

Whenever I'm angry at my grandmother I think
    She thought she was doubling my wishes with her own.
Sympathy: the sadness you think already exists.
    Sorry for your sorry.

It's not fair to be mad, is it?
If Grandma had asked me
    *What do you want? What shape
    do you wish to take?*

I would have said *kaleidoscope.*
    Chameleon.

I want to be what's right, whatever right is
    in that moment.

I WANT TO CALL MANDY AND I CAN'T

because I realized something
I had only glimpsed before:

this is for the best.

The best I can do is give the beast
some space.

The best I can do is give it
what it wants.

All its whispers:

                                    what if you...

warning me
always flashing ambulance-bright

Its silent voice has altered the course
of my sister's life

has fastened my father's eyes
on the trees outside

>   (I remember riding on his back once,
>   scream-laugh
>   *Toy Story* pajamas)

has turned my mother into Lycra
and bones

>   (I remember my head against the once-
>   softness of her arm
>   my first ride on a plane.)

Hyena laugh

Skeleton eyes

What else will I poison

if I get too close?

THOUGHTS ABOUT LYCRA

There is something stretchy
in my brain between the Lululemon
that my mother wears

and the too-small
shoes the world is always
trying to force
onto my feet.

I can't put my finger on it—
the way it all feels
connected by spandex threads

like wearing those clothes
isn't just being
the right kind of woman
but performing "woman"
right.

WHEN YOU CLOCK IN AT WILDWOOD

it's like the day after auditioning for a play.
The list is on the wall and you see
where and who you're going to be that day:

Ferris wheel, *do not rock the gondolas*

Tilt-A-Whirl, *keep your limbs inside at all times*

Bumper cars, *do not get out of the car until the ride is over*

Balance between peppy and stern,
teenager telling other teenagers what to do—
no one minds if you're nice enough.

Because I'm a good liar I'm good at faking
the nice. I tell myself it's good practice:
alien walking among earthlings
    pretend pretend pretend

But when I clock in and go to the list
I see my name beside the Loco Loco

and I'm reminded that pretending only goes so far
pretending is a house of cards
and its paper foundations
have been shaking for a while.

THIS IS THE PART WHERE I'D CALL MANDY.

This is the part where I would walk
circles into the rug at home—
the fabric beginning to wear
white with the constant tread
of my feet.

Counting, counting, counting.

But here, so many people:
the break pit full of vapers
children fluttering like birds
purple Wildwood polos swarming.

Sometimes I can barely hear myself,
like the part of me that's still trying
is getting smaller and smaller:

    You could ask Megga to switch

It all seems impossible.
The crocodile whispers: *and what about when she asks why?*

It's so easy to hurt someone
children's bodies flying into space bones
breaking the metal crumpled smoke rising me
watching and feeling nothing

I can't explain.
Explaining means being seen.

LEAH LIKES TO DRINK AT PARTIES

but I've never
liked parties either way, except once last year when Leah begged
me—this was the night she and Cesar got together, but we didn't
know that at the time. All we knew

was that it was winter
and the band kids were having a party, and the band kids always
have the best music. Leah needed me to go, needed me there to
remind her to relax her face, to remind her to dance.

I wasn't this bad yet
the crocodile was an egg that cracked every now and then, released
something red and murky. But Leah reassured me, Mandy
reassured me.

It snowed
and she drank whatever it was that Marlon was offering at the bar in
his parents' basement, and when she gave me a few sips, I felt my whole
chest burn. Looking back, maybe it was the crocodile's egg scrambling

because I danced
that night, even more than Leah, who got bold enough to talk to

Cesar and then never stopped, but I was okay because the scale-rustling noise was drowned out by the burn in my chest.

It snowed
and Leah had her hand hooked around the back of Cesar's neck
while they danced, and I was so deliriously happy for her, that she
talked herself out of doubt and into the arms of the cute boy with
the dimple

and I was delirious, too,
about all the room in my body that the alcohol made, how it
silenced the hissing and let me hear the music, how there was so
much space inside me for things like joy

things like breath
and full-throated laughter. Even with the drink, I remember that
night, and it makes me aware of how much I don't remember,
memories that pass through the crocodile sieve and disappear

into the black hole
always expanding inside me. I remember it was snowing, I
remember being warm, I remember feeling like happiness was fairy
dust that I could embody if I only stuffed enough of it into a sack.

It's this memory of snow
and warmth and music that sends me over to where Ms. Linda is
unlocking the concession stand, where I slip her little silver flask
out of her purse and up to my lips, and when she glances my way
and raises her eyebrows,

I just shake my head.

NOT A GOOD IDEA

but also the best idea because although I'm not *very* drunk

the body that always feels too big and too wrong now exists in a
separate realm from my brain,

a fuzzy curtain between me and the crocodile that lets me walk
through Wildwood with my arms swinging.

1, 2, 3, 4, 5, 6

1, 2, 3, 4, 5, 6

I ignore Mandy's texts. I ignore the thrashing tail.

With the haze of alcohol, I can ignore everything.

1, 2, 3, 4, 5, 6
the Loco Loco rattles and squeals
the children laugh
the sky is blue

I could do this forever—
    everything predictable and warm
    nothing crashing through the wall of my skull
    my smile real and easy

Summer sun like the light in a microwave, Earth turning under it
like a hot plate.

I drink bottle after bottle of water and Ms. Linda drops off a
hot dog.

This feels like seventeen should.
If I didn't know better, I would think Leah was on the other side of
the carnival
spinning cotton candy, sneaking pink tufts of it into her mouth.

It's 1:30, then it's 2:30, and the hot dog has soaked up the alcohol
and I realize too late that this is what Ms. Linda intended.

WHAT DID I DO?

It's too soon for a hangover—
the sudden throb in my head
isn't that: it's a meteor

and just like that, the house of cards
            peaceful morning,
            warm-blooded day
                        is leveled.

A dam bursts, and the crocodile
rides in on the wave:
What did you do? How could I have been so stupid? Alcohol
numbs the brain, curbs inhibitions. For the last ten months I have
been barely in control and today I left the booth entirely—what
did I do? **What has been done? And what if none of it can be
undone?**

SOMEONE IS CALLING MY NAME

and by now I recognize the voice of Ruth and through the throb
and the reptilian haze,
her voice sounds like a siren.

What's the matter? What's wrong?
Did something happen?

Something happened.

The something
is me.

I CAN FEEL MY FEET BLEEDING.

I want nothing more than to get on the bus
    where I used to think my best thoughts
and ride it across the city until
it delivers me to calm.

But the bus is no longer an option—
    and for an instant I feel something besides fear:
    anger, instead, that this is something else the crocodile has
    taken from me—

I run past the stop, too close
to the people waiting—they curse
and grumble but I'm already gone.

The too-small shoes want to devour
my feet, bones and all
but there is too much of me.

On another planet my phone
is ringing in my pocket
and the noise in my head screams
that it's the police, that I should answer it
and be done
give in
tell them that you tried, you're so sorry

But what if they're like Mandy,
so convinced that I'm good?

Helping me means helping the beast
and at this point we are inextricable,
its blood and my blood
swirling in the same veins—

whatever I was
is less important
than whatever it is
I am.

THERE WAS A PARK WHERE I USED TO GO WITH LEAH

when we were eleven—endless
green fields and baseball diamonds
a walking bridge that snaked over
the river where barges moved trash and steel.
I was there because love had turned me
into a person who liked baseball.

Felicia Palmer, shortstop—
older by two years,
one of the first girls
to start rolling her shorts at the waist
showing more of her legs
long and brown as a Thoroughbred
and just as fast.

Leah lived three blocks away
and we would walk over
chewing gum and trading hats.

I would always bring my sketchbook
do still-life portraits of catcher's mitts
empty popcorn bags

and when it was me and Leah alone
in the bleachers, sketches of Felicia—
the way she scowled and crouched low
when the batter tensed,
the way she threw her hat off
when her team won
a personal celebration before
she would sprint to join the dogpile.

She died one day, a Wednesday—

AND BEING IN LOVE, I WAS THE FIRST TO NOTICE.

In the sky the sun was half hidden
with the promise of night rain, and Felicia's team was down.

I had accidentally learned about baseball in these trips to admire
her and had learned how her team counted on her, how her talent
was fireworks the way it awed people, bright and furious.

So when the pop-up ball sailed in her direction, all eyes were on
Felicia, but being in love, my eyes had already been on her and I
had seen what no one else had:

a sudden jerk of her neck, as small as if she'd felt an insect land on
her skin.

And then she was so still.

Somehow still when the ball arced through the air

Still when she should have been running

Still when the ball cracked down into the grass seven feet away

Still, somehow, even when she took one lurching step toward the
dugout.

Then still also as she fell on the field.

Not *on* the field, *into* the field. A fall I've never seen before, because everyone I've ever seen fall was alive, and by that point, I learned later, Felicia was already dead.

When the coach and her family swarmed the field, Leah was standing up in the bleachers beside me, everyone's mouths open except mine. Me staring and silent, hands in fists, unable to unsee.

Even now I don't have to search my mind for the image: the moment her face went blank, the tiny jerk of her head, a horse twitching off a fly.

Somehow I can't let it go
Somehow I can't let it go
Somehow I can't let anything go.

SOMEHOW I END UP AT THAT PARK

I never even knew its name: when you're eleven, it's *the park*. I'm close enough to Leah's old house that stepping over cracks
in the sidewalk is like stepping over memories.

Will anything ever be the same?

And at the same time: why does nothing ever change?

Warwick Park, four diamonds, the walking bridge, dusk, empty.

And there's the diamond where a girl died, and there's where her father shouted *oh my god* over and over, and there's where her mother knelt silent and weeping

And here's where I learned there was something wrong with me,
because while her coach gave her CPR, before it had settled in that
Felicia Palmer was dead,

I sat on the bleachers and thought *I wish it was me giving her*
CPR—it would almost be like kissing her.

I RUN AWAY FROM MYSELF.

I am so tired of being in this body.

I am so tired of being in this brain.
Three miles away, Wildwood
rotates to music I know by heart
and in the center of the tune
is the rhythm of all my doubts:

what did I do what did I do what did I do

I END UP ON THE BRIDGE

and the water looks the way I feel:
metal-gray and frantic.

It's swollen with rain and all
I can think about is the artery in Felicia Palmer's head filling
with blood

sudden
inexplicable

like a curse laid around her neck.

Bad is an extra organ in my body.

Wrong is a sweat I secrete from my pores.

I think I could walk circles around Earth for the rest of my life and
nothing could stanch the blood:

> sea levels rise and with them, the swamp inside me overflowing

> until the world is filled with crocodiles, multiplying like rabbits

> pulled from the magician's hat and overtaking

> > *everything.*

I DON'T KNOW IF I WAS GOING TO JUMP—

just that I was running away from myself
and climbing up onto the rail was the next logical step.

The wind had just registered on my cheeks
eyes blown dry and hair blown back
one leg over the metal railing
the metal water calling me

> when strong arms dragged me roughly backward,
> squeezing the air out of me in one long scream.

The scream raises goose bumps.
I barely recognize my own voice—

I sound wild, obscene.

I feel wild, obscene.

I am watching myself from somewhere high above
or maybe far below, watching myself

get dumped on the concrete, hot in the sun

watching myself look up at Rex and Ruth

who stand looking down at me, one of them crying

one of them blank-faced, but neither of them

running away.

"WERE YOU GOING TO JUMP?"

I don't know.

Cut the shit, Ariel! Were you going to jump?

I don't know!

No. I can't do this shit, Ruth shrieks. *Rex, talk to her!*

How did you find me?

Megga told us to follow you. Were you going to jump?

I don't know
I don't know
I don't know

MEMORY: LEARNING VOLCANOES

I carry all its parts.

The magma chamber (where the crocodile swims—nice and warm)

The conduit of my throat, where all things travel toward the surface
        all the blood, all the thoughts that intrude like parasites

Then at the top of it all, the crater

where, if this is allowed to erupt, the lava will spill down to my body

everything in me fiery and infectious, and once it reaches my hands

all bets are off.

I'M BIGGER THAN REX

and all I can think about is hurting him

Please don't, I say when he comes closer.
Please don't, I don't want to kill you
What if I kill you, I swear I don't want to
I don't think so, anyway, please go away please

I don't recognize my voice, squeezed shrill.
Squeaky vomit, string of prayers.

Rex's eyes widen and I remember
that look, the first time I told Mandy
the first time she finally got me to talk

our room as shadowy as the inside of my head
her reading light the only glow
and bright enough on her face for me to see
the way her eyes changed
when she
      like Dad
realized what I am.

That was the day I kidnapped my sister.

I bound her hands in sisterly duty:
chaperone, guard dog, electric fence

Now here is Rex looking at me the same way
like he knows he should run but he's wondering
how fast he is, if he can actually outrun

something with eyes that shine like mine
must be.

"YOU HAVE TO TELL US."

Ruth's voice is loud and shaky—
it makes my pulse race, gas
on my fire. But Ruth
is on fire too, she walks back
and forth, shaking her hands
at the wrist:

If something is going on we need to know now
before it's too late. You're always
so quiet—are you in trouble?
Did somebody hurt you?
Oh my god you were going to   *jump*
You almost jumped.
What if Megga didn't tell us?
What if, what if, what if . . . ?

I SPEAK THE LANGUAGE OF WHAT-IF—

it's my native tongue.

What Ruth doesn't understand
is that having this conversation
is the what-if:

                    what if you let it all out
              what if the bloody lava escapes
                  the crater, what if it burns
                    everything in its path?

My phone is on the ground again
but the cracks look the same
and I guess it's ringing because Ruth
picks it up. *It's Mandy,* she says.
That's your sister right? Miranda.

Miranda, dutiful daughtersisterdoctor.
You can't be here. I'm trying

to set you

free.

RUTH ANSWERS

and I lunge, but Rex gets brave and blocks me with his body. I'm
bigger but he's determined and I can tell by his face that he will try
to stop me, that getting near Ruth is not an option and if it wasn't
for the rustling of scales I would say *thank you, please save me*

but all I can do is breathe
shallowly
like my lungs are sewn with teeth.

"YOUR SISTER NEEDS HELP."

I'm Ruth. We're here with her—she was . . .
she was . . .

I don't know what she was going to do. She's not in a good place.

She extends the phone to me but I am watching this all from below. Part of me feels like I did jump, that I'm looking at myself from beneath the raging water, my body rolled under by the waves of a trash barge and all I can think is

Good, good, that's where I
belong.

I'VE SEEN ENOUGH MOVIES TO KNOW

that the only option is a hospital, the kind
where you can't wear earrings because they could so easily
pierce the delicate veins of roommates and nurses.

Sometimes the crocodile likes to tell ugly jokes:

Would they have a gown to fit you? Borrow
from the men's ward. Something your shoulders
wouldn't snap. Monstrous girl, monstrous body,
reptile brain. Are you sure you didn't crash that
train today? Bad bad bad.

Did I crash the train? Did I crash the train?

I say it over and over
bad girl crazy girl
until I'm in a ball on the bridge
Ruth breathing as fast as the water
and just over there
the green, green square
where a girl died under my eye.

I KNOW BETTER THAN MOST

How everything's connected
How one thing leads to another
How your thoughts create your life
How attitude makes aptitude
How what you believe is what you achieve

All the things that school counselors
and church ministers have written in chalk
since the beginning of the beginning.

And this is why when Rex says softly

Tell me what's happening in your head right now

all I can do is shake my head over
and over
and over
until I get so dizzy my eyes slip shut
and don't open again for what must be
a long time.

THEY MUST HAVE CARRIED ME.

I'm laid out like for an autopsy and I hear Mandy's voice in my ear,
tinny and distant.

Ruth's face. Oak branches. Squirrels rocketing left and right above
me. My cracked phone in Ruth's hand, hovering near my face.

Ariel? Ariel. It's me. Talk to me.

The crocodile is silent, rocked to sleep on the waves of my storm.

What, Mandy?

I need to talk to you.

No, I—

I need to tell you something. And you need to listen.

SHE SAYS A LOT OF THINGS

but the scales are too loud for me to really hear—
clatter and chatter about her classes and what she has learned until
one thing breaks through the noise:

*We've had it all wrong. You've been googling violence and I've been
reading stuff about how religion can make people paranoid*

You've been afraid of what you'll do

and we've been missing what it actually is:

*your thoughts aren't a tumor that needs to be removed, an extra
personality squeezing inside your brain*

they are just that:
   thoughts, intrusive ones

that drive along the pathways of your brain, that your brain has then
turned into superhighways.

Your brain isn't full of shadows, it's full of headlights—

we just need to stop the traffic.

WHO IS WE?

I have lots of questions but that's the main one because Rex and
Ruth
are standing there listening, and if they were cats, the word *violence*
would arch their backs and puff their tails, plant questions of
their own:

Who has been riding in the car with us

Who has been sitting at this table while we eat tacos

Who has been answering those texts

Who has seen where I live

Who knows about my life

But if I could reassure them with one simple fact it would be this:

I haven't heard anything about your lives.

While you're talking, I'm counting—building a fortress
of circles and numbers
that the crocodile can't breach.

I'm circling and circling
down in the moat
until
everyone is safe.

"YOU HAVE OCD, ARIEL."

I'm almost positive. I had a seminar about it yesterday
for my psychology minor, and I spent all night doing research—

you check so many boxes and I never even knew about this:

When you spend hours googling, you're seeking reassurance
  it's a ritual that your brain hopes
  will extinguish the threat.

When you have thoughts about violence
  it's because you've tried so hard to put those thoughts away
  that it's like your brain paints it neon
  and it comes back and back and back.

The more you fight it, the stronger it gets.
You can't out-logic it.
You can't outrun it.

You don't think about blood because you want to hurt people—
you think about blood because you don't.

HOW

do you decide to tell
a secret? Maybe once
you've stood on the rail of a bridge
it's not a secret anymore.

No one is wondering *if* there is a beast—
they just need to know what kind.

"ARIEL HAS INTRUSIVE THOUGHTS."

Thank god Mandy is here
    even though Mandy isn't here—just her voice

> **You selfish, disgusting bitch. She's trying to live
> her life and escape this place and you just can't
> help but drag her backwards, can you?**

> **Black hole. Quicksand. Human cliff.**

Eyes trace the tabletop. No way I'll reach
64 repetitions here.

*Everyone has them, but people with OCD get stuck
in a loop. The loops get more and more distressing
and people with OCD can take on rituals
that they believe will prevent something bad
from happening, or sometimes to repent
when they think they have broken
what their OCD makes them believe is a rule.*

24. 25. 26. 27.

They will never understand and unless you can keep it together you're going to be alone forever.

Look at what happened to Felicia Palmer.

Leah knew what was good for herself.

28. 29. 30.

Ariel?

She's just sitting here.

"lost in thought"

She does that sometimes.

WE'RE SITTING AT THE PICNIC TABLE AS IF AT A BUSINESS MEETING NOW

instead of an autopsy. I'm no longer on the slab but on the bench, staring down at the grass and mulch through the grid-like pattern. Roly-polies, ants, go about their business. They are focused, busy, undeterred.

Like Mandy.

I'm going to talk to Mom and Dad, she's saying, her voice at the center of us, Rex and Ruth on the other side, hands folded in front of them. They are the United Nations, negotiating with the alien dropped down in their midst. I think of the movie where

Will Smith is chasing down tentacled beasts. I wish I could be Neuralyzed. Leave me blank, let me start over.

What are you going to tell them?

Everything, she says. My body feels like one insect at least: worm, writhing in the sun, seeking the dark damp.

Confirmation of all their worst fears. Dad's unanswered prayers. Brute of a daughter. Put her away. Padded room. Lock and key.

But even through the gnashing of the crocodile, terrified of discovery, the relief pierces like a tiny needle. Anesthesia. Rescue me.

I'm going to tell them they need to find you a therapist—

Dad won't let me go to therapy.

I don't care. You need someone who—

Dad won't let me go, Mandy.

Deep down he knows it won't help. He's always known what you are. Even before you did. Even the things you never told a soul. It ripples off you like a stench.

I'll make him, Ariel! You can't live like this!

Circles. Trace the tabletop. That will keep everyone safe. One day your eyes will fall right out of your head, but everyone will be safe.

He won't do it. And if he won't, Mom won't.

The treatment is effective. Cognitive behavioral therapy—

There's no point!

I'm going to fucking try, okay? Okay, Ariel? God I know you can't help it, but I can't do this anymore! You need someone to help you! Because I can't!

Rex and Ruth aren't family—they don't know the silent battle that we've been waging for so many years.

But it doesn't matter. Everyone knows a bomb when they hear it.

"I'M SORRY, ARIEL."

She doesn't need to say it, but she does
and more, about cognitive behavioral therapy
exposure therapy, words that sound like the tiny print on an orange
medicine bottle.

There's no medicine for people like you.

We can beat this together. Ask your friends to take you home, please. Are you two there? Please take Ariel home. I'll have talked to Dad by the time you get there.

WHEN MANDY HANGS UP

Rex is staring me down, but Ruth is on her phone
typing fast.
Intrusive thoughts, she reads. *Sudden, involuntary thoughts that can
be disturbing. These thoughts can be distressing for the individual, but
they do not lead to harmful action*

You never googled this?

Crocodile lashing its tail. It doesn't like
to be perceived.
It has spent these years and especially
the last ten months slowly
whittling my life away—the circles
I walk at its command
are a perimeter too,
carving out this lonely space.

Everyone is too close.

    It's not that bad, I say.

                        God, just go.

You were going to jump off the bridge, Rex says softly.

    I wasn't going to jump.

                      Good liar, bad girl.

Ruth still reading: *The thoughts can also be explicit, which can lead
to people keeping them a secret and not seeking help because they feel*

ashamed. Intrusive thoughts can be persistent and cause significant distress in some people. Often, the harder people try to rid themselves of these thoughts, the more they persist, and the more intense they become.

Does this sound like you? You should listen to your sister.

Yes I should. Mandy always knows best.

Sistermotherdoctorfriend

God, poor Mandy

Exposure and Loop Prevention, Ruth reads.

That's like what she said, right?

Ruth reading more: *It refers to exposing yourself to the thoughts, images, objects, and situations that trigger your anxieties, obsessions, and fears. Making a choice not to do a compulsive behavior once the anxiety or obsessions have been triggered is a significant step in prevention of continued obsessive-compulsive loops.*

Right now Mandy is talking to our parents. All my shadows pulled out of their circular boxes.

She's telling your father you want to kill him. She's telling your mother that you tap everything sharp in the kitchen six times before you go to bed. Everyone is safe. We can't change anything because this is how we keep them safe.

Rex and Ruth shoulder to shoulder across the table
and even now, in the middle of all this, I want
to be alone with Ruth, press my lips
against her lips, whisper all her favorite
songs into the ear with the five piercings, speed
down the highway with all the windows down.

I would get behind the wheel for you, Ruth.
I would press the gas for you.

**To kill her. You know what would happen if you
were behind the wheel of a car.**

Rex says *Let's take you home.*

His tortoiseshell eyes, warm like summer pavement, the pattern
like sun through leaves.
He talks like he's done this before, voice soft so it doesn't make the
serpent twitch.

I guess it works. Or maybe it's the crocodile steering as it always does.

BACKSEAT GOOGLING
Who needs god
when you have Google—god
never answers but Google
always does.

How can I tell I have OCD?

And Google offers a million ways to tell,
including all the things Hollywood
taught me: pencils in perfect lines
arranged light to dark. Still,

none of this is me. I am not
obsessed with anything. I can barely
finish a TV show. My room is a mess.

But then there's a section that lists other
    obsessions
that people with OCD might have:

- fear of deliberately harming yourself or others—
  for example, fear you may attack someone you
  know, strangers, or someone vulnerable, such as
  children
- fear of harming yourself or others by mistake or
  negligence—for example, fear you may set the
  house on fire by leaving the stove on

and then the compulsions:

- asking for reassurance
- repeating words in your head
- thinking "neutralizing" thoughts to counter the fearful
  or obsessive thoughts
- avoiding places and situations that could trigger
  fearful or obsessive thoughts

I feel like I'm sinking. It sounds
like me
like hearing steps in a dark hallway
and turning to see
a mirror.

It's weird to think about everything
I've lost
everything
I've been   losing
and seeing it right there
spelled out
in black and white.

It makes me turn off my phone.
The black screen feels
comforting.

Ruth looks back at me,
concern like a constellation
across her face: *What do you think
your parents are going to say?*

    I don't know.

I feel like a wildfire, my sister
digging the moat of herself
to keep me and everyone else safe.

She's so tired of digging.
I can't blame her. She wants
someone to help me, but also
she wants someone to help her.

Our parents
aren't much good
for that.

I need to get home
before the flame spreads
further.

TOO LATE—THE HOUSE IS BURNING.

I feel it at the top of the too-many stairs but still tap the knob six
times just in case
before I enter.

Inside: The father who never looks at me is standing in the kitchen
looking at me.

The mother who is always looking through me is standing in the
kitchen looking through me
but it's her that speaks:

Mandy called and told us something happened?
That you're upset? That you think you need therapy?

    I don't think—

You're having delusions, is that what you're telling us?

    I'm not telling—

Are you hearing voices, Ariel? You're imagining things?

    I'm not hearing voices.

Do you want to hurt people, Ariel? What is going on?

I don't want to hurt anyone!

Well then what is Mandy talking about? What is wrong *with you?*

"WHEN IS THE LAST TIME YOU PRAYED?"
At least
he looks at me
when he says it.

HOW DO I SAY
I can't pray anymore because it's the crocodile's favorite activity to
interrupt?
That whenever I begin
my head streams with violence

That whenever I begin with *dear god*
I hear *DEAR GOD*
as in
the moment the victim sees the knife
the moment the monster steps out   of the dark.

And what is praying going to do?

I'm asking him but I'm also just asking
because I used to try, I swear I did.

I thought maybe this was god punishing me
for keeping my eyes open during prayer
for thinking about my lips on Felicia Palmer's—
the whole inside of my head a holy red flag
to nudge me back into the lane of godliness

but the harder I tried to clasp my hands
and keep my mind clear of blood

the more it would seep in—the chandeliers crashing down and
crushing people and pew alike
and other things too: Reverend Roger with his hand beneath his
robes, masturbating under the pulpit while he reads from the Bible;
Reverend Roger picking up one of the choir girls and laying her
across the table and

me holding my breath and tracing the crown molding 64 times
128 times and whenever I would stop and pray again it would
start all over and then we stopped going to church anyway, which
reminds me

> *We don't even go to church anymore anyway* and my father almost
> flinches
> *So why do you even care?*

You're thinking about killing people, my mother
cries, and I notice *people*—Mandy must not
have told them *who,* that the *people*
I think about/try not to think about killing
are right here in this room. As well as all over
the city.

**God did I crash the train when I was drunk? Do I
not remember? What if I did, what if**

We need to call somebody. My mother
is still talking. *Reverend Roger? He will know—*

We don't need to call anyone, my father says.
There is no battle that cannot be won through prayer.

EVEN MY MOTHER LOOKS DOUBTFUL

like even though I'm nothing but a large silhouette
in her field of vision, the silhouette is now painted blood red—
harder to ignore the thing that has become more than
inconvenience
but also a possible threat.

But let's be honest—I've always been a threat
to my mother, for reasons that are like guessing
the shapes of passing clouds—fuzzy, mutating.

Memory:
Me, four weeks into weight-lifting club:
        Mr. Cipinko's advice on form and diet bulking me up—
        biceps, traps, triceps
                parts of my body I didn't know I had
                that loved to be strong, drank weight like dirt drinks water

my cousin's wedding two weeks away and my mother
telling me I should wear long sleeves

Bridesmaids don't look like that, gesturing
to my arms, when the bottom line was always
Bridesmaids don't look like you.

And that's what makes this all so unfair
because goddamn it I've *been* praying.

I've prayed to be small, I've prayed to be good
I've prayed to be small and good
and sweet and slender

and all that ever answers *amen*
is
wondering if stabbing a chest feels like stabbing a couch
or if even with the steel it's wetter

and the circles and the counting
are the only thing that works—not church

and not prayer, and even though
we're not Catholic
I've used my sister as a confession booth
and all it's done is push her toward a career
she may not even want, her whole life
oriented toward understanding her damaged
crooked kin, and even though she's trying to help

I can't help but be angry

and I can't help but stare at the father who never stares back
his eyes finally on mine
and it's worse than the not looking.

My mother is empty but he is full
of recognition, of understanding:
he has always known, after all

**Filthy broken
Evil**

You don't need therapy, he says
(which is different from *I don't believe in it*).
You need prayer.

He could say it 1,000 different ways
and still my only reply is   *Don't you think I've been praying?*

And there it is again: recognition.

Knowing.

Then pray harder.

LATER, WHEN MANDY CALLS

I let it ring and ring, cracked screen
vibrating facedown on my bed.

In a movie, my parents would be downstairs
fighting, but they've gone to dinner.

My dad gave up church for the dojo.
My dad gave up prayer for dinners.

They are always at fucking dinner.

But this is better.

This is how I keep everyone safe.

When my room feels too small
I wander to the kitchen
touch every pointed blade six times

      tap tap tap
      tap tap tap

Alone, the way the crocodile likes it.

Alone,
    everyone is   safe.

OBSESSIVE-COMPULSIVE

I know what obsessive means.
Maybe I am. Mandy asked me once

Why are you so obsessed
with serial killers?

And all I know of compulsive
is *compulsive liar*

Lies like a river flowing
out of someone's mouth
no dam in sight.

Together these words
sound like intensity
and the void where control
should be.

Maybe Mandy is right.

Maybe the god
of Google was too.

MEMORY: FELICIA PALMER

Thirteen, which seemed so old to me at the time,
me and my bony knees folded up in the bleachers
palms pressed together and shoved between my thighs.

She wasn't my first crush but when I think about her
she feels like the first everything

and all my memories
    cut grass and bare legs
    and sweat and the way her curly hair
    fell down her back like a fox's bushy tail
    and even the blanking of her eyes
    the heaviness of her falling body

it all
sews itself into a shroud that drapes over my gaze
turns the whole world ash gray.

Sometimes I imagine Felicia riding the Ferris wheel
her cap getting blown off in the wind up high
her laugh carrying down to the ground.

She didn't know who I was.
She went to another school.
I knew her only by watching,
hearing her coach shout her first name,
her last on the back of her jersey.

I don't even know where she's buried.

And it's not a matter of haunting—
I haunt myself.

The weather that day:
    barbecue weather
hot and clear, air sweet,
Felicia in the new-cut grass squinting
under her cap. It's almost
as if a cloud traveled into Warwick Park
and settled over her life.

And that's when I wonder if the gun
has nightmares about where its bullets end up.
If the knife remembers and remembers,
if poison circles the drain of its own mind, never going down.

I am the cloud over Felicia Palmer's life.
Even as I know how absurd
and maybe even narcissistic it is

to blame yourself for the death of a girl
who had an aneurysm on a baseball field 200 yards away

I have never been able to shake the feeling
that I am an omen. That somehow
the fact that Felicia's brain filled up with blood
was because I didn't try hard enough to keep everyone safe:

not enough circles walked
not enough outlines traced—
all the secrets the crocodile has taught me
to mitigate the harm that crawls in my skin
      that I didn't focus on enough.

It all started off so manageable:
6 circles at night, 6 whispered prayers
one knife-tap each.

But the crocodile is always urging more
      more
            more

and this is the first time
that I hear it and think: obsession

MY FATHER IS THE ONLY ONE WHO PRAYS BEFORE MEALS

even in restaurants. His head stays bowed
long enough to be awkward

and it was Mandy who started the habit of eating
before he was finished.

Why should we wait? she said to me once.
It's his prayer, not ours.

That's the kind of thing our father hates
and this is why he loves karate:
discipline, obedience,
and a good amount of silence.

When he stopped taking us to church
I was surprised until he began teaching Sunday morning
classes at the dojo—then it made sense: trading out
one kind of worship for another.

When I really give it thought, I think he imagines himself
as a minister. At the front of his flock, leading
them toward perfection. Every *kiai* is an *amen*
room full of eager worshippers, uniform in every movement.

This is how you get close to god, my father:
perfect unison, no aberration,
and this is why I will never make it to heaven.

THE DOORBELL INTERRUPTS CIRCLE 256

My parents are at dinner. I could just not answer
but I'll have to start over
anyway. Even the slightest hesitation
in completing one circle could risk the effectiveness
  and I can't afford that.

REX IS ON MY FRONT PORCH

He has climbed the 18 steps
and pants a little, bag of takeout in each hand.
I brought you Indian food, he says.
From Tikka Palace. I don't do spicy but I remember you do

How?

Hot sauce. Taco Bell. You chose Fire.

Oh.
I hate feeling seen.

Have you ever had Indian food?

It's my favorite.

Good. Because this shit is expensive. Can I come in?

I DON'T KNOW WHAT I EXPECTED.

Not this. Not me and Rex sitting on the floor in my living room,
vindaloo and dal spread across the glass coffee table that my
parents reserve for magazines they don't read but change out every
month anyway.
Your house looks like a model home, he says. *Like no one actually lives here.*

Not far from the truth.

I don't know how to do this anymore.
I don't know what normal talk sounds like.

My brain is staccato, punctuated by

Rex smashing his face through the glass table, my hand on the back of his head. I feed him naan with glass instead of garlic.

Stop it.

Is it all the time? he asks.

He's talking about what happens inside my head. The spotlight makes me squirm. Dark shadow of the swimming reptile, just beneath the surface.

Not all the time.

What did your parents say?

What I knew they'd say.

They're not going to send you to therapy?

He doesn't believe in therapy. My dad.

How do you not believe in something that obviously exists?

He doesn't believe it helps. He thinks it's just doctors making money off of people's problems.

What do you think?

I don't think it matters.

It definitely matters. We don't just live in the world. We have to live
inside our heads too.

WE LIVE INSIDE OUR HEADS.
Yes, we do. This world inside my skull
is small and sticky
but I live here

I have learned
the rules

I can live here
just fine
    I think
as long as no one else
comes in.

"WHAT YOUR SISTER SAID IS FUNNY"
How you both had been googling the wrong thing,
how you were so focused on what you were afraid of happening
that you missed the actual symptoms.

Like, think of how different everything might be
if the first thing you googled was
intrusive thoughts
and that was the rabbit hole you went down
instead of serial killers?

    How is that funny?

Because it's almost like feeding gas to the engine, right?
The more you read, the more you're tied to your theories
the more similarities you see

or you keep looking until you find differences

Either way you're stuck
in a loop
that winds you tighter and tighter

until eventually you snap.

HE LOOKS AT ME THEN, STOPS CHEWING.

Have you snapped?

    I don't know what snapping looks like.

Maybe thinking about jumping off a bridge

    Maybe

What would happen if I took you to a mental health facility tonight?
Mary Hodges is really good

    What?

Would you do it?

    My dad would just come get me

Are you sure? Their intake counselors are really helpful

What the fuck Rex why do you know all this shit

Remember I told you I had a brother?

NO, I DON'T.

That's the problem with the crocodile.

So often I'm so busy counting
worrying
watching myself
watching the inside of my head
tracing away all the threats—

the world becomes a muffled blur.

Memory: Mr. Dominick calling me by name six times before I
answered
Daydreaming about the top of the beanstalk?

Daydreaming about writing on the
chalkboard with your blood

How much have I missed, riding in the wind with Rex and Ruth?
How much will I always be too submerged
to hear?

"I HAD A BROTHER."

Richard, all bones, hawk-nosed brother with wild birds in his body—
when they flapped their wings my whole family shook
and when they migrated he couldn't stay in one place:

talking fast, nothing big enough to hold him but the sky
all of us on the ground shouting up, trying to remind him
that when the birds closed their wings
he would plummet

and we had seen him plummet so many times.

We didn't know how to catch him: no net,
no song, no trap would hold him. We had to be a safe place
for him to land, and when he did he would roost gently
until the birds opened their wings again,
geese flying south

exploding in feathers.

HE TELLS ME THE REST IN MY ROOM.

No one has been here since Mandy left—
Leah's presence leaking out like a glow stick lost under the bed

and that's where Rex sits when he tells me
his brother is dead.

Manic episode at Dairy Queen, stepping out of his car
in the drive-thru, teenage cashier calling the police

who the record shows spent 19 seconds
talking to Richard Gregory before firing

14 bullets into his car and body
then 64 minutes securing the scene

and never once rendering CPR.

Rex was at school when it happened
the distant island his parents banished him to
when he asked for hormone replacement.

He saw the story on Twitter first, learned it was his brother
second. No indictment.

They never even called an ambulance, he tells me.

My room is full of sirens
and all of them are silent.

I'VE SEEN HEADLINES LIKE RICHARD'S

Maybe I even saw Richard's,
this city where everyone
is some version of sick.

I know police kill people all the time
     in their driveways and on the steps of churches
     in the street and sleeping
     in their homes sleeping

in their cars sleeping
on couches sleeping

We had an assignment in school last year
special creative writing project
    the only thing I'd actually wanted to do all year
and the assignment was to write a story about a dystopia
without changing anything about our world

and I was confused. I think I wrote about people
having to steal food to survive because I knew a kid
who went to juvie for stealing lunch meat

but in class a girl named Donya understood the assignment:

gray world where the skies are filled with pollution you can't see
where people in uniforms can kill you in your sleep and
walk away
where people's bodies are nothing but incubators
where people die in their beds because medicine costs
unimaginable money
    and across the borders of this angry
    hungry country the same medicine
    is a few dollars

Medieval world
where people with mental illnesses are locked in cages or killed

I tell Rex about Donya's project
he looks at me with sad eyes.

That sounds about right.

228

IN THE QUIET OF MY ROOM

my head is loud.

Get him out of here.
Make him leave.

I know the crocodile likes me alone

You will hurt him
You will hurt him
You will hurt him
What if you do? What if you try
to seduce him?

I don't like men.

What if you do anyway?
What if he rejects you?
What happens then? He rejects
you and you get angry.
There's a stapler in your desk
You staple his hand to the wood

I need him gone. I'm wearing socks but I know
my feet are blue under the cotton.
Circles will fix this. 120 of them. More.

Have you ever tried just not doing it?

And in my head I hear *compulsion,*
straight from Google and here
in this room, in my body
and brain. But does it matter?

The *what if* is like quicksand and I sink in:
what if OCD is just   a trick played by a devil
what if   other people have OCD   but
for me it's something much worse   what if
OCD is just the mask something   worse
wears?

And this is why Rex needs to be gone.

The crocodile hates to be perceived—
bag of popcorn swelling with hot air
every kernel a tiny explosion.

I am filled with tiny explosions.

Not doing it is not an option.

Does it really matter why?

Tiny explosion. I do not talk
about the crocodile. Tail lashing the water,
everything white and furious

    No.

Why?

    Because bad things will happen

How do you know?

    I just know.

I AM A MANNEQUIN FILLED WITH BLOOD.

I am wrong inside

In my head it had become a chant and I didn't mean to say it out
loud but now he's heard—
no taking it back.

> You'll have to quit Wildwood
> He needs to warn Megga
> You can't be around children
> You can't be trusted
> You don't even know if you crashed the train

Every day my head is a train wreck
Every breath is a train wreck

I used to think that too, he says.
Until I realized I was trans.
I'm not made wrong, I'm made right.
Everything in me is right
like a lizard sunning on a rock
like a bee hovering over daisies.

And I know he means well, but when he finally leaves
and my room is dark and silent again
all I can think about is that he said *lizard*—
that my most minuscule confession
was a bread crumb leading to the reptile's den
so close he could have knocked

What if he had knocked?

Then I would have come out, Ariel.
I would have come out.

Have you ever tried not doing it?

Have you ever tried holding your breath so long that your lungs explode? Have you ever tried duct-taping your nostrils and mouth? Have you ever tried putting your head inside a plastic bag and sucking out the air?

No? Me neither.

TEXT FROM RUTH

I hope you're okay. I'm sorry I freaked out a little bit today. I know we don't know each other super well but I feel like we were becoming friends and I don't want that to change—I promise I will do better. Me and Rex are here if you need to talk

AN APOLOGY FROM RUTH

is like the smoking forest
apologizing
to the wildfire.

TEXTS FROM MANDY

Mandy: I'm guessing Dad said no
Mandy: Are you awake?
Mandy: Please let me know you're okay

"HOW DID YOU GET SO CLOSE?"

Mandy asks me this on FaceTime. She wants to know how it came to be that two strangers from the circus pulled her sister off the edge of a bridge, how they arrived with her at the edge of everything and peered over at whatever was on the other side.

I don't know, I tell her in the dark, so dark neither she nor I can fully see my face on the screen. *How does anyone know how magic works?*

THE TRUTH ISN'T MAGIC, IT'S TERROR.

Something binds the blood. Violence
in a boy's body aimed at the center
of us like a cannon. Being a target
doesn't mean you're the same,
it just means that what you're up against
is. And sometimes you have the sense
to join hands.

TEXTS WITH MANDY AFTER WE HANG UP

Ariel: he said no by the way
Mandy: I figured

WHEN MANDY GOES TO SLEEP, I THINK ABOUT THE NIGHT

last week when the three of us, Rex and Ruth
and me, sat on the edge of the overpass, land
bridge that the last mayor built so the animals
could cross from one wood to the next without
the highway clogging with corpses.

We weren't supposed to be up there but
teenagers aren't really supposed to be anywhere
and we each had our own separate rants:

Ruth: *There are a million separate wars on Black people happening*
at the same time and in Chicago it becomes two million, especially
in the summer. They cut off funding for the summer jobs program and
then they ban teenagers from public parks. Last night my friend Reina
texted me after her parents had to pick her up from the police station.
They got her for sitting on a park bench writing poetry at 7:45pm.

Rex: *My mom signed me up for a cooking class and you can't even*
make up this kind of parody. To make me more feminine, she says. To
teach me how to be a woman. She can't even make boxed macaroni
and me and my dad made Thanksgiving the last five years. So who's
the woman, Ma? It's still not me. But is it you?

Me: *Everywhere I go it's "Is that a man or a woman?" "What is*
that? Too tall to be a chick." But I know if it wasn't that it would be
something else. On the bus stop, it would be other shit for other girls.
"Nice tits!" "Take off your top!" Or "Oh, what a slut, wearing that
outfit!" No escape. Even if you hide yourself they have something to say
about that too. No escape. No escape.

"I'VE DECIDED IT'S REWARD AND PUNISHMENT,"

Ruth said. *There's a standard for women,*
right? Whatever the fuck it is. White,
thin, and hairless, and somewhere
along the way everyone decided
it was a standard that needed soldiers to carry it

street harassment like a metric
for how well I'm following the rules

comments from strangers letting me know
if I'm in compliance.

Dark-skinned Black girl, born
in violation. Red braids?
Flag before a bull.

Pink braids? Well,
I get points for trying
to be feminine
but the points never
add up to 100.

A battle I know I'll never win
but I'm given mercy if I try—

like a hatchet congratulated
for burying itself in wood
and not flesh.

"You could be a weapon but
you're choosing to be a tool."

Good girl.
Follow those rules.
Good, good
girl.

I TOLD RUTH I UNDERSTOOD

but her face became a falcon's,
bright bird eyes fixed on me.

Do you though?
The standard is you.
No matter how
you feel
the standard
is still
you.

Tall or
broad
or anything
else
you are
white
and therefore
woman.

Allowed to be tall
and still woman.

I'm dark
and therefore
already starting
behind.
Every other thing
is a strike against me:

Tall?
Tall and dark?
Tall and dark and broad?

If everything that is considered
feminine
is the opposite of everything
I am

where does that leave
me?

LONG SILENCE

until Rex sighed like an old dog.

Isn't it funny
he said
I mean, not funny.

But isn't it funny that all I want to be
is boyish? Running toward it
with my hands out like trying
to catch a falling baseball.

Why does it feel like all the things that signify
boyish or mannish
are just this arbitrary set of rules?

And they're assigned to people
who may not want them
but withheld from people
who do? Why the fuck
does anyone else
get to decide?

Why is it
never
us?

STILL AWAKE, THINKING ABOUT WEAPONS.

Ordinarily I would be up walking circles
but tonight I stare at the ceiling
wondering wondering wondering

what I might be formed against
and for the first time
what has been formed
against me.

THEY STARTED DEMOLITION ON A HOUSE DOWN THE STREET

When I left for work it was standing
and when I came back it was gone.

They will rebuild it brick by brick.
They will resurrect it in the image of the others.
It will be a clone, following all the rules.

Gazing out my window, I think what if
I took loose bricks and sent them through
every window on the block—
even our own.

I'm surprised that this thought
doesn't drip with swamp water.

It's not something I'm afraid I'll do,
it's something I wish I could.

UNDERARMS IN SOME ADVERTISEMENTS HAVE HAIR

My mom sees them and says *disgusting*.
They never used to show that stuff in ads.

We're at Target and some of the mannequins have bodies
that are fat. Photos of women with round stomachs
and large arms. My mother laughs:
What is happening?

What is happening?
What is happening?

In Target while the inside
of my head
feels full of cracks.

It's all important.

For her the earth is shaking
    Big Bang

When I'm with her it feels like the bones
of dinosaurs could push up through the earth's crust,
magnetize together, and walk the streets.

This is how the world goes backwards:

hair growing where hair grows
and my mother
    razor, comet

She calls it clean
but from where I stand watching
it looks like scorched earth.

ALSO FROM WHERE I STAND

in the aisle at Target,
womanhood is just
two dollars

extra for the same razors—
the only difference is
the pink box.

AND THEREFORE MANHOOD

is the black box with the flaming red eyes
PROTEIN TO GET PUMPED

Is this where we find gender—
in the boxes we buy?

What happens if I buy the black box
What happens if I don't buy either

What happens when womanhood is on   sale

$2 off when you buy 3

Can I buy womanhood in bulk

Can I be better at this
     girl thing
if I sign up for a Target credit card?

I'M STARTING TO THINK IT'S LIKE RUTH SAID

There is a stage and a script and there are roles
we're supposed to play. And like a script,
it's all made up. If we don't speak the lines,
the character crumples on the stage.

Every year our senior class performs *Hamlet*
and every year someone is a sleep-deprived
prince, every year an Ophelia drowns
in the pond of silver tinsel. The character
was there before the actor. It relies
on us to make it speak and walk.

And like Mr. Tegan, whose face turns red
as an ambulance, every wrong line
an emergency, the whole world is director.

And audience.
And understudy.

Tomatoes
Tomatoes
Tomatoes

Red as blood
exploding across the stage
of your life.

Don't miss one line.
Not one mark.
Not one cue.

Your life depends on
how well you play
this part.

Every stare, every whisper, every joke, every threat, every curse, every
cocked fist   a reminder.

242

Remember
remember
remember

Play this role
or   be ripped apart
or   be stoned
or   be thrown to the wolves
or   be stripped naked and burned

all while the town gathers
to grin and watch and hold hands
and break bread
all together
your punishment a thing
to be bonded over

all in agreement
that you deserve this
that they're all right

that you should've known
to

play the role
or die.

TEXTS WITH REX

Ariel: Do you ever feel like a puppet
Rex: How so

Ariel: Like . . . being a girl, being a boy, being whatever . . . we're just puppets. Playing a part

Rex: I could see why you'd think that. But the way I see it, it's the other way around

Ariel: ?

Rex: Boyhood is the puppet. I pull the strings. You know?

Ariel: Kinda

Rex: Gender doesn't make me. I make it.

I CARRY THE TARGET BAGS

from the car for my mother but I pause
on the sidewalk outside our house
listen
to the sound of sledgehammers.

Between crocodile scales
I can almost make the connection—

my mother sneering at advertisements
and the sound of hammer against brick.

What is torn down makes room
for something   else
and the something else

Looks like my mother
Looks like this house

Teeth and nails and smooth
exterior
small and clean
and same.

THE NEXT MORNING, MY FATHER IS IN THE KITCHEN.

I freeze in the doorway and he freezes at the sink.

On his chest, the Karate Kev's logo. He doesn't teach
classes anymore
just runs the office, drives the van,
talks to parents. The only time
he wears a gi is for open house

his bare feet and oak tree posture
enough to get suburbanites to sign checks.

We were suburbanites until
this house. New Karate Kev's location
four blocks away—I blush
every time I pass it,
glass-walled eyesore
logo bright and throbbing
as a cyst when I walk to

this freshly painted house
all the original rock sanded into piles

and carted away. Hollow
as the look in my father's eyes.

I'm still wearing a T-shirt and underwear
and he looks at me like I am something
sticky on the bottom of his shoe.
You can't just walk around like that, he says.

> *Like what?*

Like that.

Like this.

MY MOTHER'S WATCHING TENNIS

before she goes to tennis. She already wears the tiny white
skirt that makes her legs look long and tan, the tiny white
sneakers that make small, hollow sounds when she walks.

Highlights, she says when I walk in. She would have said it
no matter who had arrived. *All the champions from the last
20 years. Oh, I love her.* Someone on the screen I don't recognize.
Maybe Russian, maybe Swedish. As thin and platinum
as my mother.

We watch the volleys, listen to the little screams the players release—
effort and energy and force.

The clip finishes, another plays:

Oh her, my mother says, looks for the remote to mute.

    Serena Williams?

Can't stand her.

    Wasn't she the best in the world or something?

Well of course. Look at her. She should be playing with the men.

I obey, and look. Running, I can't tell.   Arms and legs. Fast.
Strong.

I'm a good googler. With this brain, I have to be.

    She's only 5'9", I say. Sharapova's 6'2".

Well, she seems bigger. I mean look.

I go on looking. But I can't tell what exactly
my mother sees that makes the woman on-screen look so impossibly
large—

her muscles
or her skin.

THIS IS WHAT RUTH MEANT
How Black girlness is like a basket
and gender is like water

one minute full: all these expectations
of feminine, unreached

one minute empty: womanhood
slender, womanhood light,
womanhood small

and yet Serena is still
a woman

Ruth is still
a girl.

Who made these tests
and if they're just made up
how can they be failed?

Which ones am I passing
just because I'm white?
And if I'm failing in part,
does that mean I'm failing
being white?

What would my mother say
if I asked her?

If I said: *When do you feel
the most like a woman?
When do you feel the most
white?*

Are the answers the same?
Are they
the same?

I'M INTERESTED IN ALL THE THINGS PEOPLE DON'T SAY

maybe because there is so much that   I can't.
When my father is silent, staring out the window
is it because his head is empty
or is there a filter as strict as mine
that keeps all the ugly odd things in their proper cages?

My mother doesn't have this same filter.

When I imagine the inside of her head
I see a school of fish so thick you don't notice the fins
        just a shifting cloud of glimmer and scale

When words flop out, they are recognizable
but the impression of what they came from lingers
        this is a part of a whole
        this was something informed by its origin

When she talks about Serena Williams
she thinks she's only talking about Serena Williams
but I have learned
        from myself
that our brains are tricky:

sometimes it gives you a piece of string to play with
and it's not until you tug
that you get to the whole   ball of yarn.

WHAT IS MY BALL OF YARN?
Still thinking about Serena Williams.
Still thinking about Ruth.

Butterflies bursting
from my belly
when I think
of her smile.

What was
the cocoon?

A girl who seems
to know exactly
who she is

or maybe hers
is a face
I just wish
I could
protect
from myself

and I want
to be close

enough
to imagine
I could.

I WALK TO FINE 5.

It's the kind of weather that Mandy loves—
warm but cloudy. The kind of sky
that gives the eyes a break.

Mandy's upset about Dad,
about the therapy I can't have.
It's hard to feel disappointed
about something you never had
any illusions of getting.

But I think about Mandy. Mandy is always   right. Mandy is
always   good.
Good   grades, good   skin. Mandy, 5′8″   the right kind of
tall. Mandy
and her pointed chin. I've never been jealous of her   rightness,
which she has held over me
like an umbrella. If Mandy says I have OCD then she's   right.

A broken clock is occasionally right,
but is a perfect clock occasionally wrong?

WHEN HARRY MET SALLY

My mother loves this movie and I've never seen it until now—
        12:30 on a Tuesday, women in their fifties

in the dark around me
laughing in a way that says they've all seen it before.

I pay close attention in movies, immersed.
Every detail is a pathway out of my head.

But today is a little different. Longing
and longing. Sally has these little habits:
ordering things on the side
liking things the way she likes them
and the man Harry rolls his eyes for 10 years
before realizing he loves her
has always loved her.

I wonder if it works like that
with things beyond mayo on a plate and not on the bread.

I imagine staying up late on the phone
with someone whose eyes are big and green
enough to love me and the crocodile too.

What are you thinking about?
    [romantic giggle.]
    Oh just what would happen if we had sex and if you can suffocate
    someone with your legs wrapped around their head

I don't know if there's love like that, wide
and smooth enough to negate the scales.

If there's love like that, I don't think I deserve it

How can a lava pit be in love, how can anyone love a chasm?

Loving me would be diving deep into ink water.

I don't want anyone to drown in me.
I don't want anyone to drown in me.

THE CREDITS HAVE ONLY BEGUN TO RUN

and I'm already steeling myself for Wildwood.
I think I should talk to Megga.

Mandy has been texting me:

Anxiety does not cause insanity.
Fears are not facts.

But what if she's wrong?

Maybe Megga should post me
somewhere where I can't interact
with the living:

making popcorn

                        What if you poison it?

or spinning cotton candy

                  What would that paper cone look
               like shoved down someone's throat?

God why am I like this
Please just go away

Ariel?

Hearing my name now, here
is like a hand grabbing my shoulder.
I jump, spin, and find Mr. Cipinko
there with a ready smile.

He's there with popcorn in his hands
while my mind is still following the word *poison*
but his bushy eyebrows say he's pleased,
that if my face is witchlike he doesn't notice.

With another teacher it might be weird
to see him outside of school, but with weight-lifting club
it's almost more weird to see him in normal clothes
and no black wraps around his wrists.

It's funny—men like him, no more than 5′6″,
are rarely the ones to turn my long bones into a battleground.

He gazes up into my eyes without minding
the angle of his neck, he doesn't try to make himself taller
or me smaller
just says

So it is you! Do you work here?

He's noticing my purple polo, which screams
employee even if it's the wrong color for Fine 5.

No, sir. Wildwood. I just came here
before I go to work.

Are you like me? I like to see movies in the middle of the day. When
you step out of the dark
and into the daylight, it's like a dash of water—slapping you out of the world
you've been in for two hours.

> *That's why I prefer going at night.* This feels like a confession. *So*
> *it's still dark.*
> *I like to stay in that world for a while.*

As long as I can.

Is this what you're doing with your summer? Movies and work?

> *Yes, sir.*

What about the weight room? He smiles. His tiny eyes on his small
face. *Do you have somewhere to work out?*

For maybe the first time in my life,
I'm aware of feeling too small.

My arms which always feel like they belong on a plastic action figure
suddenly feel scrawny.

Memory: in the weight room last year
band shirt with the sleeves cut off at the shoulders
the sticky air in the room making even the warm metal
of the bench press feel cool,
sweat like a film on my back.

Pushing hard and feeling my chest swell
tiny tears inside, already thinking about rebuilding.

I was always big but I taught myself
to be strong. And Mr. Cipinko helped.

I've fallen off lately, I admit.

Lucky for you the weight bench isn't a horse. He grins
as his partner comes out of the bathroom.
You can just get right back on—it doesn't even run away.

HIS GIRLFRIEND/WIFE/FRIEND IS KIND

and they both smile, Cipinko dropping popcorn
into his mouth: *You can always come to the school
to lift,* he says. *I'm there in the summer on Mondays and Wednesdays.*
He waves goodbye

and for some reason I want to chase him,
follow him into the dark doorway
of whatever movie he's come to see
and sit beside him in the dark
ask him to hold my hand
and tell me again what he has told me
when spotting my bench press:

Grit it out.
You're teaching your muscles
what they can do. They answer
to you when you call—grit

it out and realize
that your whole body
is in this together.

I watch his receding back,
Hawaiian print shirt—
it's like an island disappearing
on the horizon as I'm floating
out at sea.

A TEXT FROM LEAH WHILE I WAS IN THE MOVIE

Leah: I have so much to tell you. I hope you're okay.
Maybe I couldn't have answered if I hadn't seen Cipinko. But I
hear *grit it out* and answer
Ariel: I'll be here when you get back

I WALK TO WILDWOOD

and for the first time in a while
I notice how every step hurts,
how these too-small shoes
are trying to swallow me up.

I feel the curl of my toes
against the inside,
the way my bones are curving
in on themselves

the way my brain wants to be smaller
but my feet just want
to walk.

What did my grandma
always say, before she
was shocked by the size
of her grandchild?

Beauty is pain, my dear.

I walk until my feet bleed.
But why, Grandma?
And for who?

MEMORY: IN EIGHTH GRADE

Melissa Smart gave a presentation in social studies
about the women in other countries and all the terrible
things their cultures do to their bodies

for beauty
for loveliness
to be dainty and admired

neck rings in Myanmar
lip discs in Ethiopia
foot binding in China

but she never mentioned
home
    here, or

the way I've known two girls
who starved themselves into the hospital,
three girls in Mandy's graduating class
getting nose jobs as grad presents.

It seems like everyone has butt
              lip
              chin
              cheek
implants.
Carving ourselves up like deli meat
but I'm never really sure for what plate.

It's not for boys—not for me.

Why do I want to be small?
Whose plate am I trying to fit on?

WILDWOOD IS SLOWER TODAY

The sky doesn't promise rain, but it does threaten
it—a mind that could change, a passive-aggressive
kind of sky. No one wants to trust a sky like this.

This sky
reminds me of my mother.

I'M EARLY

I always am, even when I try to be late.
Memory: Reverend Roger at the pulpit one January,
speaking of the long cold months—the isolation
of winter and how it can erode the spirit. *Idle*
hands are the Devil's playthings, he warned
and this is how I know I've always been this way

     damaged, a little off, nonbeliever

because I remember thinking *that's a funny way*
of saying "seasonal depression can have you feeling
pretty low" but I guess it can't be a sermon
unless something simple gets transformed
into the battle between hell and flesh.

But I still think of idle hands when I'm early
to work, when I fail at being late. Sitting
around gives the belly-dragger in my skull
more than playthings: empty time
gives it an entire playground, slithering
down the slide while I try not to

        think about walking up to Dylan, selling
        hot dogs, taking the pointed tongs
        from his hand and jamming them
        through his neck.

The crocodile twists and turns in the slime
of my intestines. Mandy said *You don't*

think about blood because you want to hurt people—
you think about blood because you don't.

I don't know anything about OCD
but this can't be all there is—it's not a matter
of wanting to
or not.

It's a matter of whether or not
I *will*.

SINCE JASON GOT FIRED

I haven't been doing many caricatures for Wildwood—
not enough employees to run the machines,
and the machines always come first.

But this empty slot of time feels like a butcher block
so I sit in the break triangle with the pad on my lap
and my pen drifts across the page
trying not to draw something reptilian.

This isn't autopilot, this is something else.
My hand feels disconnected from my brain,

shadow puppet come to life and deciding
on a new medium. My arm unhinges

from my body and hauls itself out of the swamp.
A face appears.

Eyes dark and heavy-lidded, lashes so thick
the expression is almost sleepy. And there is the nose
lovely and broad. Lips appear, parted just enough
to reveal the gap between teeth just beginning
to smile.

By the time I need to clock in, Ruth is staring
up at me from the page, and I'm not sure how
she got there. Not anything so intrusive
as the crocodile, but a materialization of a different material.

I want to wrap myself in it
but instead I fold the paper carefully
then tuck it safely into the trash.

WHILE I WALK, I COUNT

circles of 64 that wreathe Ruth's face
salt ring to keep the witch of me away.

Ink on paper cooled the fire
but as soon as I put the pens away
the flames lick up again—

drawing Ruth fills me up with panic,
organs sloshing with gasoline.

I think of all the problems with my brain,
the doubt is among the worst

the questions I'm forced to ask myself
like

Why did I draw Ruth?

Because

    - she is beautiful

    - her smile is like a pinky promise

    - when she laughs it fills up the whole car?

Or because
the crocodile knows I want her
and it wants a map of the next thing
it will take from me?

THINKING OF LEAH

Mandy wants so badly for Leah
to be the villain.

Her silence could look
like that: white witch,
snow queen.

But snow comes
from clouds

and my skies
have been bruised
for so long.

The crocodile
wants to take everything
and it's already taken
so much.

GOOGLE IS MY FRENEMY.

I haven't looked up OCD since the day
on the bridge, in the back of Ruth's car.

It feels like a wobbly grate in the sidewalk—my mind
jumps away from it, walks around it.

What if it falls out from under me?
What if there is more to fear?

But my phone is in my hand
and my sister's words are in my head:

thoughts are not facts.

I feel panicked, edgy.
But instead of googling serial killers, today
I look up "OCD intrusive thoughts"
and find a page on a site for the Anxiety and Depression
Association of America:

Aggressive obsessions, or unwanted thoughts of violence towards self and others (sometimes referred to as Harm OCD), can be a horrifying, though common, manifestation of OCD. Like any form of the disorder, the thoughts often arise as what-if questions, such as:

- What if I impulsively commit an act of violence against someone?
- What if I lose control and harm or kill myself?
- What if I harm or kill a child or someone else I care about?
- What if I harbor a violent identity and I am going to act out in the future?

WhatifIkilleveryoneIlove Whatifmysoulisatickingtimebomb
WhatifIcantstopmyself

WhatifIfeellikethisforever

"ARE YOU CLOCKING IN OR WHAT, YOUNG LADY?"

Mr. Malcolm there at the edge of the break pit, keys
jangling. He looks at me with a dad face.

Ever since the other day, the day I went to the bridge,
he's watched me carefully, made small talk
and then studied my face with caution when I speak
like if he can catch sight of whatever it is
that slithers inside me, he can grab it
by the head before it strikes.

Yes, I say. *I'm coming.*
I just had to read something.

But my insides don't feel so slithery.
Something has smoothed into skin.

I read the last line from MentalHelp.net:
OCD isolates the sufferer, and this detachment from others, where the
person suffering from OCD is left alone with nothing but his or her
obsessions and compulsions, can exacerbate the disorder.

Can exacerbate the disorder. Can exacerbate the disorder.

Loneliness can exacerbate the disorder.

I'M ASSIGNED TO THE LOCO LOCOMOTIVE.
Because of course I am.
Skin or scale,
everything
inside me
is a wild
horse
running
too fast
and
too far
to catch.

I
am a
single
person
s t a m p e d e.

I
am
a
   solitary
          e x p l o s i o n

ONE THING THIS CROCODILE HASN'T TAKEN FROM ME

is my naivete, which is funny as hell honestly
given the ancient ugliness inside my head

but there's a lamb somewhere inside these scales
(maybe wrapped up in the coils of a python
I haven't even discovered) and the lamb
in me walks across Wildwood, heavy-footed
toward the Loco Locomotive

*maybe not today
maybe today is the day
it all stops
maybe today is new
and everything
will be fine.*

Can exacerbate the disorder.

I am eternally hopeful
and
I am eternally cringing
away from myself

because as soon as the train
begins to move I see it all happening
in slow motion:

the wheels picking up speed
around and around
again and again
everyone wondering
why it hasn't stopped
or at least slowed down
looking to the girl in the booth
only to find her watching
snake-eyed
counting down to the sixth lap
smoke rising gray then black
then white then no more smoke
just fire
and screams

MS. LINDA ISN'T AT WORK TODAY

and the only other person who has alcohol
at Wildwood is Ms. Megga herself, her shining
bottle of whiskey that she saves for Mr. Malcolm
and herself on the last day of the season.

Getting it out of her trailer
would be like shoplifting a watermelon.

This

is when the crocodile
doesn't play fair:

**If you work the Loco Loco
you will crash it and kill dozens of children.**

*Then I'll quit right now.
I'll go home and never
walk through
these gates
again.*

**No, no, bad girl. Quitting would leave Megga
in a bind. She's already short-staffed. And what
will you do at home? Wait for the opportunity to kill
your father? Is that the real reason you want to quit
Wildwood? So you can go and work in the dojo the
way he always says you should? You and him in the
mirrored room, blood on the polished wood floors**

It's watchful Mr. Malcolm who sees me
when I clap my hands over my ears.

It's not a voice but it is
a drumbeat, it is a constant stream
that won't leave me

ski-masked intruder with my face under the fabric—
and under my flesh, the greenest scales.

I'm slapping my head thinking
I should stop but not being able to stop
everything always feels like it's going to stop
once I stop counting but it never stops
even when I begpleadshout out loud *STOP* and the next thing I

know Mr. Malcolm has called Megga and Megga has called Ruth
and Rex and I'm in the zoo with the crocodile, everyone staring.

RUTH HAS HER HANDS OUT

like I'm a mule broken from the post.
Rex's face is smooth as an ironed sheet but Ruth's
eyes shine, she could cry or scream at any minute
and I don't want her to do either.
I turn away, cover my eyes.

The world is too much, and too little.
My body which always feels too big is, right now,
too small for the swell inside.

If only there were more space
an empty place inside me to shunt the beast.

I want to be alone. I need to be
alone before I hurt someone.

*this detachment from others, where the person suffering from OCD is
left alone with nothing but his or her obsessions and compulsions, can
exacerbate the disorder.*

Can exacerbate the disorder

    Can we go, I croak
    Can we go
Let's go, Rex says.
We can go.
Let's go somewhere quiet.

Quiet is a crocodile meal.
Same as noisy. Same as air.
I realize—thunderclap—that it's not going to stop
eating until there's nothing
left of me.

"REMEMBER WHAT YOUR SISTER SAID?"
No I don't.

No she doesn't.
There's nothing anyone can say
that will make sense to a brain this gnarled.
Don't you get it?
Run! Run like she's a bomb!

You can't outrun it
You can only face it

Is she on drugs? Megga asks

She was drunk yesterday, Mr. Malcolm says quietly, sadly.

There is no secret left in me.
I'm a vulture-picked pile of bones
everything bleach white and obvious

She's not on drugs and she's not drunk
She's having a mental health situation

Rex knows these words so well
and guilt careens in as large and heavy as the panic.

Breath short and rapid blinks

Oh god heart attack
Oh god my body attacking itself
Oh god crocodile like virus in my blood

I can't pass out. I can't pass out. Because what if I don't pass out,
what if I merely go unconscious

murder movie, velvet sheet between my mind and me
Ariel sleeping and the crocodile running free
in Wildwood
destroying everything in its path
starting with the train.

Take her home, Megga says softly like I'm too far away to hear.
I guess in a way she's right.

REX IN MY EAR

Let's walk together. We're going

somewhere quiet

where you can chill. Everything

will be fine. Everything is fine.

"EVERYTHING IS FINE"

Reading about whatever might be wrong
with me is like looking at a cartoon
of a dog and thinking you've met a real one—

flesh and blood
fur and howl.

There is so much more to this than they have
googled, and so while we walk to the car I try to tell them
but my teeth are chattering and my lungs
are still too small for this body
so all I manage is

> *You don't understand*
> *You don't understand*

And by the time we've reached Ruth's
car the tears have disappeared from the corners
of her eyes. She is stiff and straight as cornfields when she says

Okay so tell us. Make us understand. We can't help if we don't know.

And I want to say *are you sure*
but it's too late for that. It all spills out

RUTH, I HAVE SEEN BLOOD SPILLING FROM THE CORNER OF YOUR PERFECT LIPS

I've watched a razor split the skin across your throat in a long
clean line
My mind is ravenous
I tell myself I'm not hungry
that I'm not a hunter
that all the things
that pass behind my eyes like a movie reel

are a devil's inventions
but it's never enough.

Prayers are useless—each one is like a bread crumb
trail leading to the center of me,
luring the crocodile out from the deep.

Ruth, it's never enough. Rex,
it's never enough. I've seen you die on the Ferris wheel, I've seen
you crushed in the gears of the carousel. I've seen my hands around
knives and hammers and broken glass

I can't get in your car.
What if I reach up and circle
your throat while we're going 80 mph?

What if this is the crocodile's last wish?

RUTH STARES AT ME A LONG TIME.

Her eyes are full of scales—
not the slithering kind
but the weighing kind.

She looks at me the way my father does sometimes before his eyes
wall off:
wondering, comparison, and in both cases I don't know what
I'm being compared to.

I'm expecting her to close the car door that her falcon hand
has opened, jump in and speed away—

but instead she jerks her head at the entry and rolls her eyes so they
flutter like butterfly wings

Girl if you don't get your ass in this car . . .

Non-threat. Love language.
When I slide in, the door thuds closed behind me, sealed so tight I
can no longer hear the music from the Loco Loco.
I close my eyes and lean back, try not to see or think. Maybe if I
stay completely still
everything will slowly fade

to black.

"WHERE WE GOING?"

Ruth's already driving, my eyes are still closed. I can tell by her
voice she's looking at Rex.

He ponders for a while and then: *I think I know a place.*

WE LEAVE IT ALL BEHIND.

We drive until the wind is too loud to hear my thoughts
Ruth steering her electric time machine and blowing through
space to the moments before things went bad.

We don't stop until Rex announces *THERE* and Ruth
doesn't ask questions, just guides us silently down a ramp
into the green mouth that called to him.

It's a field, peeling red barn in the far-off distance. Miles
and miles of the everything-kind-of-nothing that is nature.

Can we be here? Ruth says before she turns off the car

Rex: *It's a nature conservancy. Public property.*

Let me rephrase, she says. *Can I be here?*

We'll hear anyone coming before they get close enough to ask.

It's good enough and he's right: it feels like we are at the center of
quiet,
the grass all bending in the same direction when the wind runs
over it—
smooth and round like sand dunes.

    Why here? I ask.

Because there's room.

DO YOU REMEMBER BEING HAPPY?

Ruth nods at Rex. To him, there is room
for all of us and all the bigness that we are,
all our sad everythings and the wide-winged futures
Rex and Ruth imagine for themselves.

When I think of my future it feels like a crawl space.

I don't need this much sky—
all my dreams have cramped shoulders.

So when Ruth lies down in the grass and breathes
the sky into her lungs
and Rex follows
I just stand watching.

My body is big and stiff—
they look so small there in the ocean of grass
and it's like Ruth reads my mind:

We're like ants she says.
This earth makes me feel so small.

You're not small to me, says Rex
and my heart aches
because I want to tell her the same thing,
want to tell her how often I shrink
then expand, then shrink again—how in some light
we're big and in some we're small
but my tongue isn't small or big—it's nonexistent,
even when Ruth pats the grass next to her and yells
at me to come lie down and look at the clouds.

So I do because it's all I want to do
even though
all I want to do is run across the grass and never stop
until I either become it
or take off into the clear hot sky.

Do you remember being happy? Ruth says when I'm beside them,
when the tops of our heads make three sides of a triangle.
Before you knew that the earth was dying under our feet?
Before you knew there were things scarier than witches and monsters?
I remember, says Rex. *I remember running barefoot and never
stepping on glass.*
I remember lighting sparklers and never getting burnt.
Maybe it's the rolling wind that draws it out of me—
it feels like the words might disappear into the air:

> *I remember holding hands with my friends and not thinking about
> cutting their wrists. I remember having sleepovers and not thinking
> I'd kill everyone while they dreamed. I wasn't always like this.*

> *I wasn't always like this.*

"YOU DON'T HAVE TO BE LIKE THIS"

Rex says. *We can help.*
He's thinking about his brother, I know,
and I want to say

> *Richard's gone you can't save him*
> *I'm not him and he wasn't me*
> *Your hand is not a lifesaver*
> *I am not worth saving*
> *Ruth's car isn't really a time machine*

But maybe it is
Maybe he can
Maybe I am

"BUT HOW?"

I'm asking Rex and I'm asking the clear blue sky
and I'm asking Ruth's hands
    which she holds up against the clouds
    using one thumb to block out the sun

We are ants
    the sun is too big to even comprehend

We are giants
    we can hide it with one finger

We are everything at the same time.

If an entire star can be held in one hand
    then a monster can be a girl
    a crocodile can be a cricket
    a Volkswagen can be a time machine

I can be good.

It's all about
perspective.

REX CALLS MANDY FROM MY PHONE

and my sister picks up, breathless:

Ariel, hi, are you okay?
I stepped out of class. What do you need?

And I reach to grab it but Rex shrugs me off

Hi it's Rex, he says.
Can you tell us the plan?
I think she's ready to try.

MANDY SAYS A LOT OF THINGS

Exposure therapy: remember, you can't out-logic this thing. OCD
    is mutant logic.
You will make a maze around all the fears but
as soon as you blink, the OCD will have transformed
the whole thing, restructured every twist and turn and laughed
in your face. Remember: you can't escape it, you can only face it.

Make a small list, she says, *of the   top three things*
that have been impacting you.

Which in my head translates to *what are the crocodile's three favorite*
meals?

Exposure therapy sounds like waking up the crocodile
on purpose
then refusing to follow its orders.   Terrifying.

She says it like it's so simple.
Like this is a matter of choosing the tap
for cold water instead of hot:

    No ketchup.
    Blue, please.
    Turn left

one of any million banal choices,
a decision that doesn't involve life or death;
just snapped fingers and a thumbs-up.

Mandy is good. Mandy is always right.

But what if she's not?

She says OCD is the doubting disease,
that its presence in the mind will make you
question everything you think you know.

Running over an empty can in the street—*did you hit someone? Did you commit vehicular manslaughter? Are you sure that wasn't a person? What if the cops are looking for you as we speak? Go back and check. Then go check again. Count to 64 once for every mile you drove away from the scene of the crime. 7.4 times. Better not to drive ever again. That will solve this once and for all.*

Doubt is an extra organ in my body. Does making this list begin the process of excision? Is this something that can be removed or is it enmeshed in every cell? At what point do you become more crocodile than human?

THE LIST

- Bus stop: pushing someone into oncoming traffic
- Home: doing something to hurt my parents (especially my dad)
- Wildwood: hurting someone
    - But mostly   crashing the Loco Loco

MEMORY: IN ELEMENTARY SCHOOL

making dioramas of a scene from a book that we loved: shoebox cut out like a stage, pipe cleaners and glue sticks and whatever else, we were supposed to do it ourselves.

I spent two weeks cutting out cardboard animals, coloring them with markers, arranging them with the most precision I could wring out of my nine-year-old fingers. Glitter. Pom-poms. Glue.

And when it came time to bring it to school, I was so proud— carrying it on my lap on the bus and smiling even when I had to reglue one of the people when I got to class.

And then I saw everyone else's.

Lauren's with 1,000 beads glued in perfectly symmetrical rows
Tara's with tinfoil and gold paint in alternating strips
All the dioramas with the craftsmanship of gods

Too shocked to cry. I presented mine in a mumble while Lauren Cheshire-catted. It wasn't a competition but I can still feel the realization in my chest, like a pill stuck low in the throat. My best is not enough, there is something essential I am lacking that comes easily to others. I am perhaps delusional about what I am capable of. My high hopes are so often dashed by my own hand.

I tell Rex and Ruth this because the sky drew it out of me, because I don't want them to be disappointed by my inevitable failure, my inevitable falling short of expectations. They are betting on a horse with lead feet.

I don't expect Ruth to laugh, but there she is, lying in the grass chuckling.

You think those kids did that shit? Their parents did it for them, goofy! Lauren or whatever-her-name-is's mommy had a glue gun and a box of tinsel. They should have failed!

They were like 9, Rex laughs.

Fuck them kids, she says and then I laugh too.

No way my mom would have helped me, I say, and like the small-massive sun, these words feel both big and small. The urge to protect her is sudden and unexpected. *I mean, it's not like I would have asked her though.*

Imagine that, says Ruth. Then she squeezes my hand.

WHILE WE DRIVE, RUTH TELLS US THE PLOT OF HER NEW SCRIPT

See there's this guy who works in a deli and everybody drops their business cards into the cookie jar, right? To win free lunch or whatever. And the guy starts to keep track of all the people who are rude as fuck and he looks up their businesses and stalks them from those and then, obviously, kills them based on who's rude and stuff, you know? He's like the anti–customer service survey. Or something.

Does he eat them?

Why would he eat them?? She looks in the rearview at me, alarmed.

I can read her mind. She's wondering if this is something I hadn't mentioned in the list. If this is something I'm thinking about right now. If her one arm out the open window is being imagined
    on a long baguette

I am already regretting this, this project, this attempt . . .

Don't disappear into your head, she says. She smacks the steering wheel. *Stay here.*

BUT WHAT IF . . .

Like Hannibal Lecter. Because he eats people who are rude, you know.

Ohhhh. Shit you're right! My guy is like the working-class Hannibal.

What if he killed them at their jobs, Rex says. *Like you come to his job and act rude so he comes to* your *job and kills you.*

Ruth and her elf grin. *I like it.*

WHAT IF

What if he goes to a guy who works at a bakery and orders a cake and then goes out to his car and poisons it and then comes right back in and says it doesn't taste right, *no really, eat this and tell me it tastes normal to you.* And the guy he wants to kill says *fine* and takes a bite and the poison is slow-acting so he doesn't drop dead until he's home and then

I KEEP THAT TO MYSELF

even if part of me itches to tell Ruth because I think it's the kind of
thing she would laugh at: she and her razor brain, always looking
for characters, always looking for something that makes her grin
wide and her eyebrows high. *Stories.*

But once you have admitted things like what I have admitted
    my list on Rex's phone
there are new rules that govern what you say.

Saying nothing is still ideal.

Counting circles at home is still the best bet.

All this will be okay as long as
I can keep
everyone safe.

OCD IS THE DOUBTING DISEASE

but I have a hoping disease too.

If she was afraid of me and my scales
would she have told me about her script?

Would we be riding in this car
fast and faster into the almost-sleeping sun?

I always sit behind Rex so I can see the curve
of Ruth's cheek, the way it rises when she smiles.

I doubt anyone could ever love this thing
that I am, but as the dusk whizzes by, violet,

I am sharply aware of the kernel of hope
hidden deep in the doubt, shrapnel

waiting to escape from its cave and surge
on its bloody path toward my heart.

TEXTS WITH MANDY

Mandy: so you're going to try

Ariel: I guess so

Mandy: you have to be sure. You have to commit.

Ariel: what do you mean, commit?

Mandy: you have to love yourself like a marriage. You can't quit,
even when it's hard.

Ariel: so divorce isn't an option

Mandy: okay actually yes divorce is always an option. And like,
maybe more people should use that option. Actually, marriage was
a bad analogy. Fuck marriage. You have to love yourself like you'd
love yourself if you loved yourself, does that make sense?

Ariel: Um . . . NO?

Mandy: Shut up. Everything is up to you, Ariel. But you deserve to
be happy

Ariel:

Mandy: I said you deserve to be happy, Ariel

Ariel: hmm

"DESERVE" IS A LOADED TERM

and maybe if I was as smart as Leah or Mandy
I could write something about how I hear *deserve*
every day from a million different mouths:

> You "   " *a vacation.*

> You "   " *the best.*

> She "   "*d it.*

> Get the respect you "   ."

> I "   " *to splurge.*

> He "   "*d better.*

It always feels like there's something missing,
something unsaid. Where does this deserving
come from? Earned? Inherited?

And who decides?

"CAN'T WE START TOMORROW?"

Let's not put it off.
It's going to take practice.
We'll be with you.
It will be fine.
Does it matter which bus stop?

No it doesn't matter which bus stop.
The only factor that counts is my presence.
The bus stop could be inside a church
        and it wouldn't matter.

Church. Prayer. Bread crumbs.
I already feel the scales twitching—
this is how it starts
and they still don't understand.

        Do I?

PANIC

My body is flight.

I open the car door.

One look

at the innocents

living their lives

transforms

me into shudders.

I can't move

lungs heaving

even air

feels like

violence.

I breathe

bad.

JUST LIKE THAT, I FAIL. WE GO TO THE DRIVE-IN.

It's been closed for two years, parking lot and screens empty, weeds pushing through the gravel,
    reclamation.

Why did it close? Ruth wonders. We sit on the hood of her car, staring at the place where I watched *Wreck-It Ralph* when I was six.

I look at Rex because he always seems to know everything but he just shrugs.

Dunno. I loved this place.

Ruth is silent, cross-legged between us. I can feel both of us leaning in, wondering, but Ruth isn't the type to wait to be asked. I love this about her, that silence isn't a tool. When she's quiet it's because she's not ready to speak. And when she is:

This place makes me think of my cousin. I miss her. She's been gone for two years and I wonder how long I'm going to walk through the world noticing all the things she would've loved. Am I going to spend the next 80 years bookmarking all the things I'll tell her about in heaven?

I wonder if Rex already knows about this. If this is one of the things that's been discussed while I was present but not present, counting or tracing.

Rex asks: *How old was she?*

Pia was eleven when she died. How does an eleven-year-old think of suicide? How does that even happen?

I know when to be silent and so does Rex. Far ahead, the movie screen is dead, blank, but I still get flashes of all the stories that could be, flickering across its surface. Rex and his brotherbird, Richard, Pia watching from heaven, me and the city of bones inside my head. We are three graveyards inside a graveyard. What can we do but sit and mourn?

MEMORY: THE FIRST TIME I SAW FELICIA PALMER

It had just rained and the fields were muddy but the teams played anyway. Me and Leah were there because it had been storming for three days and we had to get out of the house.

Turn left off her porch and wander.

We got there when the team was first trooping onto the field, everyone high-stepping, hating the mud. Except one girl, marching to her position, socks already splattered.

Posture like a ballerina, cap backwards.

I already knew I liked girls, but she was a hot stove on a winter day. She was the confirmation of everything I felt in my bones. A baby goose raised by humans seeing a flock for the first time:

yes, yes, there I am, that's me up there, flying.

TEXTS WITH MANDY

Mandy: How did it go?

Ariel: I think you're overestimating me

Mandy: Explain

Ariel: you're trying to reform something that can't be reformed

Mandy: Jesus, Ariel, you're not the police. You're a kid who needs therapy.

Ariel: Kids do terrible things

Mandy: what have you done that's so terrible?

Ariel: it's not what I've done, it's what I might do

Mandy: but that's the language of OCD, isn't it? I'm still learning, but it seems to me that it tricks you into thinking you're a danger to others if you don't follow the rules and rituals it feeds to you. So you keep doing the rituals because of what *might* happen, and nothing ever happens, and you think it's because you're doing the rituals, but the fact is, you wouldn't hurt a fly.

Ariel: Better safe than sorry.

Mandy: I've been studying this stuff intensely for days now, and what you just said is basically the foundation of the OCD brain.

Ariel: Maybe you should be a therapist.

Mandy: Yeah, maybe I should. Dad would LOVE that.

WHAT I DON'T SAY:

I saw your essay, the one
that got you into college—

worried about the church
pushing your sister
away from the light

heaven and hell
and virtue and sin

twisting in my mind
like little porcelain devils.

Are you relieved?
That what's in my head
isn't a devil
but a . . . what?

A loose screw?
A squeaky wheel.

What do you think
about the church now?
Do you still find yourself
wanting to pray

or have you started looking elsewhere
for answers?

WHAT I DON'T SAY: PART 2
I killed a girl.

I didn't pull a trigger or plunge a knife or close her throat

but my wrongness is a swarm of hornets

that I let fly into the world

and I don't know how it works

only that I watched her breathe

and I watched her too closely

and then I watched her breath

stop.

GROUP TEXT

Rex: The summer feels like it's almost over
Ruth: It's not.
Rex: School is like an assassin waiting around a corner
Ruth: Five more weeks. That's a long time.
Rex: Compared to what?
Ruth: A breath, a minute, a shake of a lamb's tail
Rex: lol what
Ruth: There's all the time in the world.

LESS GROUP TEXT, AND MORE

Ariel eavesdropping on two friends
who are falling in love.
They know I'm there of course
they added me
but I have the sense that I am their alibi
my non-presence allowing them
to say the things they're still
too shy to say into each other's ears

and this is another guilty scaly thought
maybe the only one that comes purely
from my own brain and not the reptile within

but I'm glad Ruth is going back
to Chicago, back to her dad,
even if it means the void she will leave,
the ache I already feel.

Back to her home and me to mine
and Rex to his, so I never have to see
the moment that they kiss.

"ARIEL WHY ARE YOU SO QUIET? ARIEL WHAT'S ON YOUR MIND?"

If it's not blood and broken glass, it's numbers.
What's on your mind—37, 38, the shape of the car window . . .

Now I have to start over because you spoke to me. The sequence
must be complete or the protection won't work. If my mind
wanders, if I stumble between numbers, I have to start all over.
This isn't magic, this is surety. If there is a doubting disease then
this is the only thing that's
        certain.

THINGS I WOULD LIKE TO SAY TO RUTH BUT NEVER WILL

When I think of wind
I think of you.

When I think of wild horses
I think of you.

When I think of hawks in the sun
red-tailed
wide-winged
I think of you.

I think of wild and wondrous
     you
whenever I look
at the night sky
and catch far-off lightning—

brilliant and unexpected,
too electric
to touch.

MANDY CALLS

and calls and calls.
It's the middle of the night
and I wonder if somehow she knows—
if sister senses travel across miles and states.

But as always I am split between two desires:
     help me, and help you.

That's the ugly truth of it:
that when Mandy packed her things for college,
I watched her go with a sour surging relief.

I don't often sleep, but before she left
I didn't sleep at all:
     always afraid of what I'd do if I closed my eyes
     my sister just 10 feet away, dreaming and oblivious
     to the lizard in bed across the room.

So I ignore her calls. I know she wants to help.
I know she believes what she says.

But there is an algebra to this equation, balancing both sides:
    she believes what she says and the outcome is saving me.

I believe what the crocodile says and the outcome
    is keeping everyone safe

The more important of the two
is as obvious
as the fangs in my mouth.

TEXTS TO LEAH I NEVER SEND

1. Have I always been like this? When you think back
to the day we met, all the windows of the bus down
and the wind reaching in, do you remember noticing
something off? Was I another problem that you
thought you could fix?

2. How are you so good? How do you always know the
right thing to do? Does a shadow ever cross your
heart? Do you ever feel your teeth in your mouth and
wonder if they bit down hard enough, if they could
tear the flesh of a person's neck?

3. Am I good, Leah? Do you think I'm good under all
this? Do you think I'm okay? Tell me all the ways I'm

good, please, like you used to do. Please be my
lullaby. Please put it all to sleep.

4.   I'm sorry, Leah. I'm sorry for the way I am.

TEXTS TO LEAH I DO SEND

Ariel: I have a lot to apologize for when you get back
Leah: No you don't

SHORTER IS SAFER

The less I say, the less I say.

THIS HOUSE SUCKS.

Lying in my bed as still as possible so I don't wake up the beast.
Memories are tricky because
      like prayer
they can become bridges: rumination like a road paved with lava
right to the bright hot center where everything burns.

So when I allow memories to leak in—they have to be specific
and one that comes up a lot is our old house.

Memory: a yard thick with trees, the fence swarming with ivy.
Bird nest on my windowsill, tucked against the gutter. Some birds
return to their same nest again and again, the intricacy of twigs
and mud built to last. I never bothered it, knowing better.

Memory: house with no stairs, everything flat and opening into itself, one room into the next; but corners, lots of corners. Kitchen brown and warm, tucked away and overlooking the leaf-covered yard.

This new house has a different logic.

No yard except the postage stamp of scrubby grass, the smooth wooden deck eating it all up. No leaves because no trees. I imagine the birds flying right over, bird vision scanning this patch of land and finding nothing that spells survival.

Stairs and stairs, a house that grows straight up. Few corners: everything open to itself. The kitchen with no walls, whatever is being cooked can never be a secret: if toast burns, the whole house is black bread.

My life collapsing into Mandy's. Two rooms to a shared room. Why move to this house where we have less space? *Simplify,* my mother said. But things are only ever more complicated.

I don't know how much houses cost but I know this one costs more because lately everything costs more—it's the only thing that makes my mother smile. They go to dinner and dinner and dinner. The kitchen never smelling like anything because no one ever cooks, not even to burn toast.

We are smaller and closer and farther away from each other than we've ever been.

But this is where they wanted to be. Six dojos meant something important. My mother getting smaller and her smile bigger and more like broken glass. My father looking at me in the big white kitchen and then averting his eyes like from a solar eclipse. I burn his retinas. The rightness of this house only makes me more wrong.

And this is why memories are dangerous. Because now the crocodile is gnashing its teeth.

> You are Wrong. This is how you stay Right. Climb out of bed, drag your wrong body from the covers. Walk circles onto this brand-new floor until every drop of your cold blood has returned to its human state.

I couldn't sleep even if I wanted to.

I WAKE TO THE SOUND OF SHOUTING,
open my eyes, confused and flailing—
I don't remember falling asleep.

The voices are my parents, and this stupid, open house makes it
easy to step outside of my room
and look down over the ledge at where they stand arguing in the
too-white kitchen, lamps like prison
searchlights pooling around them.

You can't just call the police on everyone you see, my father is shouting.

I can if they're doing something wrong, she's screaming back.

It's a goddamn hassle, Melody! Why is everything always a hassle?

They've always done this, even before all the dinners. A little alcohol greases their throats, all their stiff dry gears whirling into motion, turning the wheels that lift the screams out. Mandy was right—this is why you can't love yourself like a marriage. It's in the script but why should it be? And why should we read those lines that make our throats do this?

I deserve to feel safe in my neighborhood, Kevin! We don't all know karate!

You could if you gave a shit about learning how—

Oh, fuck karate, Kevin! I shouldn't need karate! I should feel safe in my neighborhood!

You're the one who wanted to move here, Melody! You practically insisted on it with the Realtor!

If Mandy were here, she would be leaning over the rail and interrupting, calling them both on their bullshit. She always made it look so easy: ears like X-ray, seeing the bones of an argument. It's not so easy for me: I get stuck at the skin.

But I try.

> *Someone's going to call the police on* us *with all the screaming,* I call into a lull.

Heads snapping up, Mom glaring fuzzy-eyed.

What did you say? she demands.

> *Why did we move here if you're scared of it? You can't just call the police on everybody. For all you know they were one of our neighbors.*

Don't start that woke bullshit. I thought we'd get a rest with Mandy gone. My father is good at talking to me without looking at me. It makes me want to scream at him until the whole world falls apart and there's nothing left but my face.

It also makes me want to disappear, every wrong inch of me.

MORE SHOUTING

Dad drunker than I thought.

He's never hit me but

> *memory*

> such a far memory, blurry like a distant star
> standing in the doorway of my sister's room
> old house, little me
> little her
> Dad shouting, Mandy crying
> his hand raised but never connecting

> space between them growing
> Dad backing out of the room shouting
> moving past invisible me

his hand not connecting
Mom somewhere down the hall

all of us never connecting

now the distance still growing,
his eyes missing me
and me missing him.

TEXTS WITH MANDY

Ariel: has Dad ever hit you

Mandy: a couple times when I was younger. You probably don't remember

Ariel: I might. I don't know.

Mandy: why didn't you answer my calls

Ariel: Idk. I don't have anything to say

Mandy: I talked to the professor who teaches the course for my minor. She gave me advice for you. I told her Dad doesn't believe in therapy and she said there are things you can do by yourself. There are books you can read.

Ariel: Books.

Mandy: you know how to read Ariel

Ariel: knowing how and being able to are two different things

I CAN READ.

But I can never stay inside a book—
my mind crawling out of the pages,
the words blurring as I withdraw into my head

never trusting myself: *did you actually read*
those words? Do you actually know what they mean?

Sometimes I think the only way to live in this world
is to do it while asleep:
cryochamber, Rip Van Winkle, Sleeping Beauty

Maybe I need my parents to piss off a witch
Maybe I need to search this half-city for spinning wheels
        prick my finger and stay endlessly asleep.

As I lie in my bed thinking
and trying not to think
the realization creeps up through the mattress,
grips me like a night terror—

the crocodile is happiest when I'm alone

even happier in those times when I can't
commit any transgressions, which is to say,
        asleep.

The realization is as soft as cat feet
I feel the hint of claws with every step:

It likes me alone, unconscious.

                        It will not stop until I'm dead.

THIS IS THE FIRST TIME I'VE GOTTEN MAD IN A LONG TIME.

It takes me a while to recognize the feeling
shivering up through my bones and rattling my teeth

This is bullshit, I whisper into the dark.

This is bullshit bullshit bullshit

MEMORY: RIDING THE CITY BUS FOR THE FIRST TIME

I learned from Leah.

Some mammals are ready to walk the moment
they drop down out of their mothers' bodies

That was Leah: new horse, deer unfolding its legs.

She has been seeking independence since before
she knew the name for it
everyone else pining for 16, learner's permit:

*Why wait for that? I can get where I want
to go now. Public transportation is free and better
for the environment.*

Her parents, loose leash, always encouraging
her, seeing her, pushing her along.

We were thirteen and traveling across the city
getting lost and googling schedules
pretending not to see the old men and their wolf eyes.

Anxious Ariel, nervous at first, but opening
up to the freedom like butterfly wings,
soaking it up like lizard on noon-washed rock.

We wandered every corner, even places we shouldn't
have been. Fearless Leah, brave and bold best friend.

Yes, you're another thing the crocodile has taken from me.

RITUALS

Ever since Mandy said that what I do is ritual
I can't stop seeing it everywhere—

not just in the way I count
or walk circles
or trace windows
or even google serial killers

but things outside the scope
of what she calls OCD.

Wearing shoes that are too small
even when I bleed

Wearing clothes from the girls' section
even though they're never long enough.

Making my voice higher when I talk to men
so they don't think I'm one of them

Where did I learn these rules?
Can I play a different game?

WHEN I THINK OF PUNISHMENT

I think of prison. Or a ruler
across knuckles—old school. The church
ladies loved to say *spare the rod*!

As in, don't spare it.

I risk something
when I make my voice climb

when I wear clothes
that make my body
feel chained—

the trapped feeling,
an anchor strapped
to my back
while trying to swim.

But to choose the alternative?
I risk something else.

I know what will happen—
the looks I will get

from mother and stranger
alike.

The strange hostility
from adults in public
spaces.

Men always
trying
to chew me up.

What I risk is bigger
and half-visible
when I break
these rules.

And so is the
punishment.

WHEN I PASS THE PLACE WHERE ME AND LEAH

used to stand when we would catch the 6 to the riverfront,
I feel something inside me leap—not the lizard,
but something soft and furred
or maybe something with wings, brushing
up against the dark room where I store memories—
    the good ones

There's something about a bus that is magical:
stepping inside a moving space

sitting down and closing your eyes
and, by doing nothing else,
opening them and finding yourself
someplace new.

What if?
What if I?
What if I could?

Can I outrun myself? Can a bus go fast enough to leave myself
behind?

I've been still too long. People have arrived.
A man with gray in his beard, a woman
and her small child. Oh god her small child.

Small child, massive truck
The trucks get higher and higher and children
are always small
Easy to shove that small body out into the street
red truck and red blood
and me red-handed, red-hearted watching blank-
faced while the mother weeps
why why why

The only answer is "me."
1, 2, 3 . . .
It begins
    but it doesn't begin
because it never ends.

"GET IN LOSER WE'RE GOING SHOPPING!"

Leah would have already had her Mace
in her hand but it's not Leah—it's just me,
made slow by my inner battles.

So I don't Mace anyone, I just turn and find Rex and Ruth
grinning curbside, Tempera the Volkswagen
halted quietly in its electric hum.

We had a feeling you'd be walking

We figured we'd come and scoop you up

We. It makes my heart cringe. I don't know
if it's the idea of Ruth with someone else
or the fact that there's yet another *we* that I can't fit inside of.

You're going . . . shopping?

No, Ruth says shaking her head. We *are going shopping.*

RUTH WANTS TO BUY FRUIT.

*In Chicago I used to go to the farmers market every Tuesday before
school*
even when the polar was vortexing
even when the wind was Chicagoing

*Me and my cousins waking up early and taking the train all the way
there—*
    six girls, six hungry girls.

Pia liked plums and grapes, anything purple
my alliterative baby cousin
eating it all down to the pit.

Three of us in charter schools
Three of us in public
breaking bread at the market before funneling
ourselves toward our individual destinations.

When it was warm, I would get cherries because I could make them last—
one in my mouth before class and play with the pit until the bell rang.

I'd meet Pia at her steps after school with that tiny stone still in my mouth
and only then would I spit it out.

Big-eyed baby cousin—my auntie always telling me to take care of her
but no one really had to tell me. She was my baby bird.

Always smiling when I picked her up.

I never had a clue.
I never had a clue.

I DIDN'T EVEN KNOW THERE WAS A FARMERS MARKET HERE.

Turns out Ruth googled it, hungry for juice and core.

It's down by the river, white tents spread out in a small city.

Rex buys her cherries and we sit, down by the water
on benches carved into the rock banks.

Ruth takes tiny bird bites, eyes on the water,
nibbling until her fingertips are stained purple.

I know how it feels to be hungry
for something that you can't eat.

When she gets to the pit, she stares at it for a while before
giving it to the river.

"LET'S TRY AGAIN BEFORE WE GO TO WORK"

We all clock in at 12, the hour in front of us big and empty.
I know without needing to ask that Rex means the bus stop
again.

His grief makes him stubborn.
It makes me shy.

Losing horse, broken putter.
Don't bet on me, you two.

But he insists,
she insists.

Rex: *I know it's complicated but it's also simple.*
It sounds like you have to prove it to yourself—
like a trust fall.
You have to fall into your own arms.

Say it, Ruth says, to me. Watchful Ruth.
This is why I'd stayed away from her: she's all eyes,

the eyes of someone who missed signs once and will never miss
them again
Whatever it is. You don't have to keep it inside.

It hisses out:
> *It's not me I'm worried about falling.*
> *It's about who I push.*

I don't think you'll push anyone. Prove me right.

THE BUS STOP ISN'T BUSY THIS TIME OF DAY

Everyone going somewhere has already gotten there—
mostly teenagers like me
bullshitting or going to bullshit jobs.

But there's always elderly folks—
men and women slow and creaky.

Old people are always going somewhere.
Even my grandmother before her death
was always calling my mother and yelling
at her to take her somewhere: doctors and malls
and social calls and grocery stores.
Full calendar

and the old woman on the bus stop today
is no exception, standing with her bag clutched
because the two boys on the bench don't have the sense
to let her sit. But the bus is coming and she's creaking
forward and Rex and Ruth are watching me from the car.

I'm standing there like a child at a spelling bee
shaking and lime-lit.

The bus is coming and I am there and this old woman is there and
the panic is already twice her size, it unfolds its wings—oh god the
crocodile has grown wings—and warns me

> How dare you even take this risk, you're betting
> on yourself like this is a horse race when you
> are a fucking dragon

I RUN

too-small shoes eating my feet
and all I can think is

good

good

take it all
make me disappear

eat
    me
        alive

I'VE NEVER BEEN A FAST RUNNER

too uncoordinated—not just
that my limbs are too long
but somehow too many of them

I want to be small and quick
I want to be fox and not elk
I crash down Broadway
like a moose through a shopping mall

I don't know what I'm looking for
a refuge
a burrow
or maybe just
another bridge.

MEMORY: THIRD GRADE

parent show-and-tell, Millie's mom
is a doctor and has come to tell us all about her job, all the people
she makes well every single day
She has brought her doctor kit and all its tools, lets us pass each
silver instrument around,
        cold and shiny.

Then she shows us how she takes someone's pulse and what
it means—
the heart thumping inside the body like a party, she says, though
she doesn't mention that all parties end.

She asks for volunteers, and back then I was still the kind of kid who
volunteered for everything, my hand in the air like a schooner's sail

Four of us, all of our hearts lined up waiting to be heard

Mitchell, then Donovan, then Lula, then me

Such healthy hearts, she says of the boys. *So strong and clear.*

When she listens to Lula she smiles and laughs: *You have a heartbeat like a little mouse. So quick!*

Lula and her bony body, proud of her small quickness.

When the stethoscope is pressed against my chest, I feel its coolness through my T-shirt. I hope it sounds like a party someone wants to be at. A party of mice.

But I am fourth in line, the last child before Millie's mom moves on to the next instrument and time is ticking and she is realizing she should have chosen two volunteers instead of four so she withdraws quickly—

Very good, she says, a quick smile and a pat, and I must have always been too sensitive for this world, because even now, moving like cement down Broadway, I can remember how it felt in my chest to stand next to a girl with a heart like a mouse and have it all come together in my mind:

It would be better if you were smaller.

WALKING, I PASS

my school. It's Wednesday, Cipinko probably
inside there with wrists wrapped,
mustache twitching while he lifts

and lifts
and lifts

If I am in a hole
even if the hole is   myself
maybe I need only lift myself out.

I need only
          lift

I KNOW THE WAY TO THE WEIGHT ROOM

Behind the school, tucked away like a wardrobe
that leads to Narnia. Except instead of snow
brushing fingertips, the smell of sweat
spills out in invisible drifts.

I peek in the door, just to see.

There's Cipinko, wiry as ever,
a fan the size of a bass drum humming
from its residence in the corner.

Cipinko holds court. Three boys,
two with bodies like birds
fine-boned and narrow,
the other large and soft
as a folded quilt. They listen.
Cipinko talks:

What are you
looking for? What are you hoping
to get out of this?

Hidden, I don't answer,
but the boys do:

Boy 1, bird-bodied: *muscles*

Boy 2, sparrow-boned: *I want to be as strong as my brother*

Boy 3, large and soft: *I'm tired of being fat. I just want a good body.*
This feels like prison.

Cipinko tells them all the same thing:

Bodies are not bad or good, the only
thing they are is ours. We can't be trapped
in what is ours.

BUT THAT'S NOT TRUE.

That's not the only thing they are.
Are they? I want
to go in, I want to sweat through it
while I ask myself these questions.

But I want what these boys want—
what they're allowed to have and I am not:

I want to watch my muscles stretch
and grow. Bigger. Stronger.

More.

I am not supposed to be more.

Cipinko can't be right because a body
is more than our own.

This body is not just a body but a   blade.

If a body is a prison then can it also be a   key?

I used to think that something must be wrong
for my mother and my father
for men on the street
women in locker rooms
to constantly remind me of my body's
violations

but ever since Ruth sat with her legs
dangling in empty space
rabbits running behind our backs
over the bridge built so they wouldn't die

I can't quite shake the feeling that
    violation
could mean prison
but could also mean a shortcut into

freedom.
5'11" and broad-shouldered
feet like a giant's

parts of me are already outside the lines

what would happen, where would I
end up
if I turned toward myself
     not away
and kept walking?

IT'S NOT UNTIL I'M LEAVING THAT CIPINKO CATCHES ME

He comes out for water, sees me turning away.

Ariel! Not lifting?

He doesn't ask why I haven't come
before. I'm always grateful for the kind
of adults who know that some questions
have answers that are too complicated
for casual afternoon asks.

     Not today, I say.

Something is bothering you.
He didn't ask it as a question,
so I don't have to answer. I'm thinking

about what the boy with the quilt body
said. I ask Cipinko:

Do you believe the body is a prison?

He smiles widely like he has been thinking
of the very same question, or like he's been answering
it in a diary and is glad to speak it to the air:

How can it be? When our minds
are free? And brain exists in body?

    But all these rules, I argue. *All these*
    things you can't be. All these
    standards only a few of us will ever meet.

You answered your own question. We walk
together. The weight room stays open, humming.
I could go in if I wanted to—lift forever. He says:
The rules are the prison. Not the body. The body is just
a place the rules think they have jurisdiction.

    So I can opt out, I say, laughing.
    I can unsubscribe. Choose my own adventure.
I did, he says.

    And you're happy?
I'm free, he says. *If the body is a war zone,*
it is also an escape pod.

I TRY TO ESCAPE, BUT I JUST END UP AT WILDWOOD

Even when in crisis my sense of duty sits on my shoulder
like a pirate's parrot, balanced by the devil that's always on the
other one.

No room for angels here.

I go to the break pit but it's filled with smokers,
no space to walk my circles, no quiet to count through.

I'm still thinking about the child on the bus stop,
how the crocodile's path feels greasy: how it slides
up into the sand of nightmare so easily.

Mandy says there's ways to fight this
but they all slip out of my grasp.

I walk quickly to the Ferris wheel and find Linda
running the booth. Her eyes make me want to cry
the way they mother-crinkle, concerned. She barely
knows me but maybe she knows a beast when she sees one.

You need something? she asks me, afraid of the answer

She thinks I've come for her flask but all I want
        is to go to the top.

SHE CAN GIVE ME THIS.

Send me to the sky
where everything is small
and big at the same time.

The little carriage takes me
up and up, each one having
its turn to be stopped at the top.

Linda knows which car I am
and gives me extra time.

It's safe up here.
I am like the bomb in Batman
when he flies it high up over the ocean
where its blast can't hurt anyone.

No breeze today, barely rocking,
I could stay up here forever:
mind clear, hands empty.

Please, Linda, let me stay.

Maybe a mental hospital wouldn't be
so bad, maybe it's just the place
for someone like me.

Maybe the thing I've been fighting to avoid
would feel something like peace.

RUTH IS WAITING ON THE GROUND

How did it feel? she asks me.

    Good.

Did it help?

    I guess so.

Wish you could jump on a Ferris wheel every time you start to spiral

    Yeah that would be nice

Megga says you're doing portraits today

    Okay

And I'm supposed to sit with you

    What, why?

Maybe I can be your Ferris wheel

"WAS IT ALWAYS LIKE THIS?"

The question she's really asking is
Were you *always like this?*
and the answer is
    yes.

"NOT TRUE."

The voice in my head that sometimes is bold enough
to whisper:

Not true.

At one time the thing in your head was harmless.

Repeating black cat
Pink sweater
Lyrics to Alabama Shakes

things you didn't ask for but didn't
necessarily mind.

And then they grew
and yes that's your fault
because who else's would it be

but it wasn't always
like this.

I SKETCH A DOZEN FACES

I'm out of practice but it comes together
Nose after nose
Mouth after mouth

I get lost in all the tiny secrets that make a face—
scars and wrinkles and birthmarks.

Memory: drawing my sister in the backyard of our old house. She's
sleeping in the hammock, one arm over her eyes and the other
hanging down to the grass like a vine.

In my mind, locusts buzz
and mosquitos land
on my calves
before I slap them away.

But the memory fades, replaced
by the face before me who sits
on the stool asking to become paper.

I'm sure there's something in the science,
something that says distracting the brain
is good medicine, that even if art can't silence
a storm, it can quiet it.

But what happens after?
What happens when they get up?
What happens when the chair is empty?

If OCD is the doubting disease then what
kind of doubt is this, the always anticipating
what happens next, what happens after,
what happens when the crocodile stirs from the lull?

And just like that I'm counting.

I'm so good at this
    at keeping people safe

I slip into numbers
like a warm bath.

"HOW DID YOU GET SO GOOD?"

Ruth asks when I finish a color portrait of a woman and her
boyfriend. The caricature part is getting easier: an eye is an eye,
whittled down to its basic parts.

I like this: finding the most beautiful part of someone's face and
making it huge. Turning
an interesting nose into a feature attraction. A face is a carnival
its ups and downs, its unique music.

I've liked drawing since I was a kid, I say, putting all
my fancy markers back into their places.

My cousin Pia liked to draw, Ruth says. *Except she liked charcoal.
Her hands and nails would always be covered in it. Streaks on her
clothes. One time she went to school with a smudge on her nose.
The kids were relentless.*

Kids are brutal, I say. I know that firsthand. *I'll never know why.*

A lot of kids' first bullies were their parents, she says.

The roller coaster clatters by, too loud for us to hear each other, and
in the noise I consider that:
parents as bullies.   What we get is what we give.

I've never thought of my mother as a bully. But she says the things a bully would.

The quiet after a roller coaster buzzes. Ruth thinking about Pia. *When some people get hurt, they just hurt themselves more.*

"HURT PEOPLE HURT PEOPLE."
Sometimes people
  is she
    sometimes it's we
      and sometimes it's me

WHEN MEGGA COMES BY AT THE END OF THE SHIFT
she asks me how it went.

  Fifteen faces, I tell her.
  And one dog.

Someone wanted a caricature of their dog?

  Yeah but it was really just a portrait.

Nice. She does the math.
Fifteen faces and one dog . . . 22 minutes per face give or take. Not bad. See if you can get it down to 15 minutes per face.

Time is money, Ruth says.

Yes. Megga smiles. *But time is also life.*

TIME IS LIFE

I do the math while I sit watching
Ruth and Rex pop balloons with darts.

Last night I counted to 64
64 times
then walked 64 circles
then lay down and had to get up
and do 64 more because I thought
about   kissing Ruth
but I stuttered on 61
so I started over

Four hours of that.

Then an hour of sleep, then
up to pee, then
64 more because I heard my dad walking down the stairs to the
kitchen

           **and thought about following him out
           and pushing him down all twelve**

Then bed.

Hours. Hours of my life.
The crocodile swallows the many minutes up
gray tongue wet and eager.

I watch them throw darts,
remember what I did or didn't do to Jason
dart in his thigh

this isn't in the script

I still don't know
and I can feel the crocodile wriggle,
hungry to eat up more
of my life.

INSTEAD OF FEEDING IT, I TEXT MANDY.

Ariel: what if it's not OCD? What if this is something else, and
thinking it's OCD makes things worse, like blowing through warning
signs, and in the end I end up hurting someone? What if it's just that
I'm sick in the head and it's not OCD at all?

Mandy: or what if it is? You've read the links I sent you. There's even
memes that talk about exactly what you're going through. What if
it is OCD and avoiding dealing with it just prolongs your suffering?
What if you asking these what-ifs is just a ritual?

Ariel: I'm not the one who's suffering if people are at risk

Mandy: but what if they're not? Don't you see that right now, that for
a long time, you are the only one who's hurt?

"SAY IT OUT LOUD."

I'm still sitting there, and jump
when Ruth and Rex sit down
on either side of me, heavily like sacks of mail.

I'd been counting.
Cycle interrupted.
My body shudders—
the impulse to get up,
to flee somewhere safe
where I can count in peace
yanks like yoked oxen.

Rex's hand gentle on my arm:

Stay, he says. *Stay with us.*

Say it out loud, Ruth repeats.
Get it out of your head.

She leans back in the sun,
eyes closed, and then Rex
glances at her and does the same.

Lay it on us, he says.
Better out than in.

And maybe it's because of the sun
or maybe it's because they sandwich me,

my arms pressed to my sides,
their warm bodies like a straitjacket,
but I do.

"I'M WATCHING KYRA RUN THE BALLOON POP"

and I see all the kids coming to her counter and I'm thinking that I can't work the balloon pop because what if while I'm working I'm holding the darts and a kid is standing there with their hands on the counter waiting for their prize, and I take the darts and jam them through the kid's palm

pin it to the counter

all the small bones in the hand crushed.

They would sue Megga, and Wildwood would cease to exist and she would wonder why she ever hired someone like me, why she didn't see all the signs and cut me loose like a fish that she thought was a bass and turned out to be a shark.

I'M SO READY FOR WHAT I IMAGINE THAT I'M TAKEN ABACK BY WHAT ACTUALLY IS:

Ruth with her hands over her mouth, laughing so hard she's snorting.

"I'M SORRY, I SWEAR TO GOD"

She snorts louder, and I think my heart has stopped beating.

Memory: a prank Lula played when we were children:
I have a surprise for you. Close your eyes and stick out your hand.

Naive Ariel. Never quite
getting it.

Hand open, eyes closed,
then a moment later,
something smooth and wet
and strange—

she licked my palm,
and I was horrified
because I hadn't washed my hands
and she had just eaten Cheetos,
an orange stripe across my skin
shining with her saliva

me standing there, open-palmed
not knowing the proper response,
considering slapping her
but running away instead.

Crying only in private
and not quite sure why.

I stare at Ruth, who goes on snorting,
and it's like a tongue on my palm
except minus the revulsion
because she's so beautiful
when she laughs, but more
importantly—
she's still here.

"ARIEL, PLEASE, OMG!"

I'm sorry, I'm so sorry
because that is so fucked up but also
hilarious *because Ariel*
be serious
you would never do that!

You would never do that.
Remember what your sister said?
You obsess over it
because it's something
you don't *want to do.*

You know how much fucked-up shit
I think about in a given day?

If the inside of my head
was that empty drive-in,
all the thoughts
up on the big silver screen,
people would get torches

and pitchforks
and burn the whole thing down.

The inside of my head is a slaughterhouse
and a pinball machine
and sometimes it's a brothel
but I'm weird, you know?

We're all *weird.*
We're all
so
fucking
weird.

"IT'S NOT THE SAME."

I have seen the change in my own sister's eyes, in the moment she realized
that the thoughts weren't fleeting sailboats skimming over blue water.

Here, think:

pirate ships, waterlogged, Spanish moss hanging from the bow
dropping anchor at the center of an inky sea. That
is me.

But Ruth just shakes her head, and Rex pushes up off his knees,
looking across her to stare into my eyes:

Have you ever thought that maybe you're *not the ship? You're just* on *it?*

"WE NEED TO TRY AGAIN"

Ruth says, *right now.*
And before I know it
we're driving, Rex pushing me
into the front seat even though
I'm afraid I'll grab the wheel
and send us all off a bridge

but I don't have time
because we're pulling over
at the first bus stop Ruth sees
and she leans over to open my door

This time, Rex says. *You can do it.*
Is it a voice you hear? Say I'm not listening to you.
Tell it I don't care what you say, I know
I'm not going to hurt anybody.
These are just
thoughts.

Get on the bus Ariel!
Get on the bus.

THIS TIME OF DAY

There's a small crowd: seniors and a young mom, two teenagers sitting far apart. Older man in wheelchair. **I could grab its handles, push it straight into the path of the bus, would anyone stop me? Would I push them too? I can feel my muscles tensing, prepared for the effort it would take** . . . the dread knots in my belly.

I'm not listening to you, I think. Even in my own head, my voice is unsteady.

The bus is far down the road, slow slow slow. So much time to do what no one should ever think about doing. **You sick bitch, you shouldn't be here,**

if you run now you can get home in time to...

Beep. Ruth across the street, staring from her car. Her head is out the car window, her finger pressed to her lips, eyes huge.

I can't help it—I laugh.

By the time I stop, the bus is a block away, and I see it coming, see the man in the wheelchair, only two paces just barely out of reach. **If I stepped quickly I could do it. You monster** . . .

Shut the fuck up, I think. *Jesus, shut the fuck up.*

Bus squeaking to a stop and me waiting and not running.

The ramp unfolds from the bus like a lizard's slow tongue

But that can't be, because the man in the wheelchair is being delivered to safety, away from me

I shouldn't get on this bus. No, I didn't push anyone, but . . .

but you will

Shut the fuck up, I think. I think of Ruth laughing so hard she snorted.

I have never thought of the crocodile as ridiculous.

I pay the fare. I get on the bus.

TEXTS WITH MANDY

Ariel: I rode the bus today. I just this second got off

Mandy: how long had it been

Ariel: a long time

Mandy: I hope you're proud of yourself

Ariel: I don't know about that. But I'm happy

Mandy: you should be proud. It was really brave.

Ariel: it's not like I went on a mythical quest. I just got on a bus.

Mandy: you're fighting something you can't see, against a threat that's not real. Sounds like a mythical quest to me

Ariel: it feels real.

Mandy: I believe you

Ariel: I haven't told you about the counting

Mandy: what counting?

Ariel: it's complicated

TEXTS WITH RUTH AND REX

Ariel: What makes you feel safe

Ruth: I'd have to think about it. Not much does.

Rex: That place we went last week. The nature preserve.

Ruth: You like the quiet

Rex: and the smell. It's so clean. It lets you forget that the world is burning.

Ruth: Ariel, answer your own question

Ariel: riding in your car

Ruth: ☺

Rex: I thought you were going to say knowing karate

Ariel: lol shut up

MY DAD IS WASHING DISHES

steam rising like dragon breath,
the water so loud he doesn't hear me come in.

I stand there watching him, his broad
shoulders slightly hunched.

He's still wearing his gi. Open
house today.

Memory: him trying to convince me
to take lessons: *It doesn't have to be me*
he says, *you can learn from Jeff. Or Mara.*

   I don't want to.

Don't you want the structure? Don't you want the control?

Memory: Mandy at our old house
both of us wearing *Frozen* nightgowns.
It's Christmas or maybe Christmas Eve
and she's asking me if I still believe in Santa.

  I never believed in Santa

Wow, and I've been trying not to tell you.

  You could've told me.

I wanted you to enjoy it for a while.

  I'm not a baby, Mandy

No, you're not.

Dad coming in the room, delivering
Mandy's freshly washed gi.

Ariel doesn't believe in Santa anymore, Mandy reported.
He only looked at us for a moment. He never
stayed in our room long unless Mom was there.

Good, he says. *You're growing up.*

Then he was gone.

Now the water turns off and he
turns his body, hands bright red.

Jesus, he gasps when he finds my
unexpected presence there in the kitchen.

   Sorry.

One glance, then away.

*Is that what you wear to work? They don't tell you
your shorts are too short?*

I look down. They only look this short
because my legs are so long.

I tell him it's 98°.

*The metal on those rides is hot.
You could burn your legs.*

   I work the machines, I don't ride them.

He is far away in his head. He is never here
in this house. I imagine his mind
like a dojo: long empty room, mirrored
wall, his dream-self doing kata after kata
every movement stiff and controlled.

   Where's Mom? I ask.

She's somewhere.

He is hurriedly putting away groceries.
His hands are still red.

I rode the bus today.

I tell him because I need
to tell someone.

And nothing bad happened.

His hands freeze but his eyes do not,
looking everywhere but me. The face
of his child will burn his retinas.

What did you think would happen?

Everything Mandy told you about.

I still don't want to say it all out loud.
Behind him is the drawer with all the knives.

At some point when he has gone
to his room or the office, I will need
to come back down, tap each handle
the required number of times.

Or do I?

Prayer works, he says.
And then he's gone.

TEXTS WITH MANDY

Mandy: I know I've already said it, but I gotta say it again. Seriously I'm proud of you. That was hard, and you did it.

Ariel: I can honestly say it's the hardest thing I've ever done

Mandy: even once you were on the bus?

Ariel: I thought I was going to throw up.

Mandy: did you?

Ariel: no

Mandy: another win

Mandy: tell me about the counting

Ariel: it's like a salt ring. The right number means everyone will be safe. If I do and don't do the right things, then everyone will be safe

Mandy: except you

Ariel: I'm not NOT safe

Mandy: but you're not free either

Ariel: no

LONG TEXT FROM MANDY

Mandy: I spoke to my professor again. I think I'm going to change my major. Religious studies can be my minor. I'm just . . . so into this psychology stuff? But anyway, she told me to tell you: don't expect what you're doing to solve all the problems. It's really not meant to be a replacement for real therapy. But maybe if you can just hang in there until you graduate . . .

IF RIDING THE BUS

was like pulling teeth,
then stopping the circles
will leave me gummed and bloody.

I have always understood this as prevention
    strategy
    wartime   defense

and every day
is battle.

The rules demand
I visit the knives first.

The house is dark and silent
my parents in bed
or at least in their room
and I make my way to the kitchen
like the enemy I am.

Drawer full of silver killing

I stare down at each blade lit by moonlight
and something feels different—
sadness like a layer of dew on night grass.

I hate all this.
I hate all this.

I'm so tired of this.

BUT THERE ISN'T AN OPTION.

My parents are in this house with me
and I feel my wrongness at bone level.

For a silver moment, staring at those knives,
I wonder if I could cut it out of me:
if the thing that makes me this way
is a tumor I could cleave, meat from skull.

For once the blood would be mine.

But Mandy.

    Mandy
    Mandy
    Mandy

Mandy and all she's done
Mandy and all she will do
Mandy left alone to stare at the stain
and think she didn't do enough.

What if the wrong isn't something inside me
but something on me

something putrid that has settled on my skin,
a layer of invisible grime?

I tap each knife six times, in moonlight
my hands as silver as the blades

then I turn the kitchen sink to scalding
and wash as long as I can take it.

TEXTS WITH RUTH AND REX

Rex: do we all work today?
Ruth: yep
Ariel: yes
Rex: good. I have an idea

JEALOUSY

Not just the way that he makes her laugh
but the fact that he doesn't make her.

Ruth has a spine like steel—there is nothing she does without
wanting to

and that makes this feeling even sharper.

Not sharp: dull

A dull ache when she throws her head back to laugh when he says
any old thing

A thump in my stomach like a slow-motion punch
when they meet eyes and he can look back without
wondering   what she'll see

I AM PREPARED TO WALK

but when I'm almost to the bus stop
I hear the bus itself roaring down the block
and I think

> Why not
> Why the fuck not

I've done this once:
nothing bad happened.

I have completed my circles
I have counted without mistake
I am as safe a person as I can be
I can get on this bus and not draw blood.

THERE IS ONLY ONE PERSON ON THE BUS STOP.

A girl my age, braids down to her butt.
She has in headphones.
She taps her fingers on her thigh.
For the first time I wonder
if it's not a rhythm she's tapping out
but a matrix of numbers sewn together like salt

If instead of music she hears the sound
of infants crying
the brakes of speeding cars

if she counts her way through it
each tap like dodging raindrops.

This time Ruth and Rex
aren't across the street watching
me like mobsters, and if the crocodile
respected a witness
it thrashes its tail now to remind me
that I am unsupervised, unobserved,
and the panic rises like noxious green swamp

so close to the top of my throat
that I think I really truly will vomit
right here by the shoes of the girl
who is now stepping to the curb to signal the bus.

This is the moment where I push her
This is the moment where you push her
This is the moment where I push her
This is the moment where you push her
                    where you push her
                    where you push her

**and it's too late to count and it's too close to
stop this is the moment where you push her in
front of the bus what if you kill her what if you
only break her leg what if her mother is the
mayor what if you watch the tires crunch over
her body like a mannequin**

or what if

and these words come in Mandy's voice
they come in a shade of pink
so different from the blinding white of the crocodile's teeth

or what if
you don't?

What if your brain
is   lying?

And I am so surprised by the emergence
of these words
that I don't notice
the bus is squealing to a stop
and the girl is getting on

and everyone in the windows looking at me through the glass
not because I have just committed murder
       but because I'm making them late for work.

THE BUS'S KNEELING FEATURE IS BROKEN

An old man needs to board
with his massive suitcase
and by now
there is just me
and the girl with braids
two elderly women
a teenage mom and her baby

When I rise to help,
the old man waves me off.

He wants to manage.

But I can do more
than manage.
I lift the suitcase
place it on the bus,
hold it while he pays
the fare.

He doesn't say
thank you but
it's okay.

I am far away—
I am remembering
how it feels to stand
inside my body

Remembering the way
the gym smelled when
Mr. Cipinko corrected
my dead-lift form

The slow whir
of the fans above
like the wings of geese

Leah bought me
weight-lifting gloves
for my birthday

They're still in my room.
black and nondescript.

Memory: wearing them
for the first time—
transported into myself,
seeing myself
in the mirror
with an empty space
shaded in.

I don't think this is in
the script.

Nothing in this world
could make me small—
shrinking is a power
I do not possess.

But I can grow.

   I can grow.

REX'S LAST TEXT

said meet him at the darts and when I arrive, he and Ruth are
already there, lounging against the counter.

I remembered what you said, he tells me. *About imagining putting the
dart into someone's hand.*
It's just like the bus. Let's sit here until you see that you can't do it

That she won't, Ruth corrects. *Because I'm pretty sure Ariel* can *do
whatever she wants. It's just whether she will. Whether she actually
wants to. And she doesn't.*

I look at Rex so I don't look at her.

**What if she thinks I'm some kind of pervert
staring at her too long what if I stare at her
mouth what if I grab her breast right now here
in front of everyone what if she presses charges
and I'm labeled a sex offender what if**

Come back, Ruth says. *Stay here.*

Do I love her, or is this what a dog feels, towed up
from the bottom of a well hanging from a bucket?

Ruth knows drift
when she sees it:
she knows when someone is carried away
by a current she can't see.

I'm here. I can't look at her to see if she believes me. It feels
wrong to see her.

All the wrongness in me looking at all the goodness of her.
Can eyes leave stains? Can just looking let all the swamp water
leak out?

Exposure therapy means exposure,
Rex goes on. *Just based on what your sister said. We don't have work
for an hour.*
Let's expose you.

IT'S NOT HARD AT FIRST.
The park has only just opened, people
bringing little kids to ride the carousel
before big kids swoop in and turn Wildwood wilder.

But then the big kids are there, streaming
in, and teenagers
and the dart toss gets busier, the sound
of bursting balloons like the white poppers
they give kids on July 4th, tiny deaths.

And with all these people, there are so many hands
to put darts through.

The blood in my heart rushes faster
and stronger, thrumming into the swamp of me.

What I don't understand
is how quickly the crocodile marks its territory.

In summers past, I have stood at the dart toss
for whole days and never had a bloody thought

but now that I have,
it's like a flaming bookmark
stuffed between the pages of my brain:

I see the darts
I see the hand
        and my mind is screaming
on the expressway toward
the moment the crocodile
saw the darts and gnashed its teeth.

Did they have to make the darts this sharp?
They are feathered reincarnations of the knives
in my kitchen drawer and I can remember
how cold and heavy they felt dropping into the trash can
before I learned that tapping and counting could keep
everyone safe.

                    This is how you can do it.

Reptile tongue.

                              New routine
                              New system
                    Gives the darts a wide berth
              Something that renders you powerless
                 if you happen to be within four feet
                                   of a dart.
                                  No, three.
                         Three is half of six.
                                Count to...

Hey, Ruth says, *are you counting?*
Don't count.
Stay here

She's asking me to stay.
She wants me here.
Or maybe she just doesn't want me gone.

Jesus we are two girls who have stood
nose to nose with death.

What is here
What is gone
What is left
    of me?

I CAN'T HANDLE IT.

Too many kids.

What if I hurt a child

What if I hurt a child

Memory: my aunt's new baby
born prematurely
and brought home from the NICU
after two entire months
in his safe plastic capsule.

Seeing him for the first time
swaddled in white muslin printed with bananas.

Do you want to hold him?

And I said yes.

No sooner had his tiny peach head
settled into the crook of my arm
than the crocodile rose from the mossy deep.

> **What if you stood at the top of the stairs
> and threw his tiny body down the whole
> flight? You wouldn't even have to throw
> him hard to kill him. So small so helpless.
> Your aunt screaming and tearing at her hair.
> Would she go pick him up what does a person
> look like running down the stairs to retrieve
> a dead baby, banana muslin caught on the rail
> and hanging like a shroud?**

What if I hurt a child? What if I hurt a child? What if I hurt
someone I love?

My god
I cannot be here with this
I cannot be here
I cannot be

MEGGA FINDS ME IN THE BREAK TRIANGLE.

I have just completed my first set of circles
and I am able to hear her when she speaks
because at least one full set is done
at least this bit of protection is in place.

She sits down at a picnic table
spins the ashtray at its center
with one pinky.

I see you struggling, she says. *I wish I could help.*

My ribs are a cage
but there is more
than a heart and lungs inside.

I wish you could too.

There is so much that I wish.
I wish my sister's words
and all her ideas
about what's wrong with me
could be injected into whatever it is inside me
that makes me this way.

Can you tell me what it is? Megga asks.
Drugs? My son struggled with drugs. If it's drugs . . .

I'm not on drugs.

Memory: the same party where I got drunk while Leah danced with Cesar—turbulent ocean smoothed by liquor. The next morning all the questions in my head like an army of sharp shelled crabs:

    What did you do what did you do

    What if you don't remember

    What if someone is dead and you don't remember

praying in sets of six, prayers like spirals, prayers like scaffold

A boyfriend? she asks. *Someone hurting you?*

Sick of me to want to say yes. To say
that anyone else is the problem.

That the blood is outside and not in.

    My sister says I have OCD and she's always right
    but it's like someone telling you
    that the animal chasing you
    through the woods isn't a wolf
    it's just a rabid dog.
    But teeth are teeth.
    Aren't they?
    All I can think is
    I don't fit—normal body normal brain . . .
    I know everybody has their little bumper stickers
    about how normal is boring and blah blah blah
    but from where I'm standing normal looks safe
    and I just want to be safe.

    I want everyone to be safe

"NORMAL IS A TRAP"

and so is humble and so is small. A trap
is anything hidden that wants to catch you and not let go

Look at me.   And I do.

You think it was easy growing up
in this body? In this world?
Wrong size
Wrong language
Wrong voice

Do you hear my voice?
This is a bison's voice.
And there is nothing wrong
with the voices of songbirds
but I am not a songbird.

Would bison ever apologize
for being too big?
A bear for being too strong?

I left home—wandered the world for thirty years
and have been big and loud on every plain

I have turned myself inside out
and my posture has been bad and good
I have lost so much of my body
that my clothes hung off my back.

*Can you imagine? Eating less so that parts of my body would
disintegrate?*

Think like a philosopher, kid!

*Why would you lose any part of yourself
to fit through a keyhole?*

Can you imagine trying *to be weak?*

Weaker? You want to throw those muscles away?

You want to be a real woman? A right woman?

Real *is a trap. And so is* right.

And woman *might be too.*

IT'S THE KIND OF SPEECH MY SISTER WOULD UNDERSTAND.

Philosophy and psychology
and I am just a girl with a brain
full of holes and teeth.

Focus on caricatures,
Megga tells me. *Do
what makes you feel safe
until you figure this all out.*

But one question: OCD?
Isn't that the thing
where you line things up
and wash your hands
and keep everything clean?
Is that what's so bad?
Is my carnival too messy?

She's trying to joke so
I try to smile.

> *No, it's not that.*
> *Your carnival is fine.*

I am a puzzle—she
is puzzled. But she's going
back to work, back
to other people
who need her help.

She says before she leaves:

No? Then what is the obsession? Maybe
another kind of perfect.

FACE AFTER FACE—
mothers and sugar-mouthed kids
a man all alone wearing a Batman shirt

girlfriends with their boyfriends
and one pair of boyfriends
who squeeze each other's knees.

When I draw their eyes
I draw them looking at each other
because even though they're staring
straight at me for the portrait
they are oriented toward each other.

Like golden statues on either end of a shelf of books,
they are in love with the task of holding each other up.

When I give them the portrait they smile and smile—
smiles bigger even than the ones I gave them
on the paper.

You really see people don't you, one says
when he pays me, tips me $20.

They're gone before I can answer: *Sometimes.*

Only sometimes,
when I'm not distracted by
myself.

I WONDER IF LEAH HAS EVER FELT WRONG

She has never been the kind of girl
that is used like a sigil on a crest
not *most popular*

and, she would say,
lacking the entrepreneurial spirit
to be *most likely to succeed.*

Not a theater kid
not a cheerleader
but rather
the kind of girl who gets things done

Girl most likely to see a room
with all the chairs folded
and begin unfolding them
in organized lines until everyone
else joins in

not because she has *the spirit of a leader*
but because she sees solutions that
once begun
others find obvious.

Girl most likely to see a lost tourist and ask
if they need directions before
they even make eye contact

Girl most likely to ask "Do you want
me to take a photo?"
for that tourist and their family

Girl most likely to cry in class
when we watch a documentary about war
and not care who sees her

Girl most likely to pass a test
but never remind the teacher
that homework is due.

Girl whose brain is neither black and white
nor red
bloody mess.

When I think of Leah I think of
perfect balance
tightrope walker strolling
above a packed town square
making it look easy:
one foot in front of the other
moving but not teetering
on the line between mind and matter.

Leah, how do you live like this?
How does your mind make
sound that isn't noise?

Have you ever felt wrong?

Wrong like brushing your teeth with a spoon.

Have you ever been a pebble in your own shoe?

These are questions I would ask if she wasn't far away,
a distance a text can't cross.

I've spent too much time
asking her other questions:

Am I okay am I okay am I okay
Am I good am I good am I safe

Only now am I starting to see
that the obsession isn't the evil—
the obsession is trying not to be.

SOMETIMES I FEEL LIKE SOMEONE SIGNED

a contract in my name.

Ariel Burns solemnly swears to have a spotless mind. She will
uphold and obey all the rules of perfect civility. She will not sneeze
too loudly. She will not accidentally step on the back of another
pedestrian's shoe on the sidewalk. She will take up as little space
as possible. She will slouch when she's in a room of short men. She
will be a girl, which is to say she will be a *good* girl. Ariel Burns,
here signed, promises to keep all her thoughts at a reasonable
volume, including her dreams. She promises to patrol the
perimeters of said thoughts diligently. She will pay all associated
fines when

in violation.

THIS CROCODILE IS A BAD ROOMMATE.

Sitting on my stool at Wildwood,
when I look at all the space I've made
for this reptile—all the people
that it has swelled out of the way—
I can't help but tremble.

Leah, all the way to DC, no line between us

Mandy, chased to Michigan to answer questions
the crocodile asks.

I didn't have many people to lose
but I look far down at the Ferris wheel
where Ruth opens and closes the gate
and even though she's going back
to Chicago at the end of the summer

I still imagine her fading away
finger by finger, braid by braid.

I wish I could fix myself in time
to make her
stay.

HANDY WOMAN

There was a movie at Fine 5 once
where two brothers buy a mansion,
inside which lives a mouse

a tiny mouse
       just one
who destroys all their attempts
       of restoration.

By the end, the whole thing
crumbles
board by board, cloud of
dust
but the mouse survives.

No matter what I'm doing
I can feel every nail and screw
holding me together.

What I'm dealing with
is so much more than a mouse
and I wonder if
       by the time I fall apart
it will fall apart with me
or if when I'm gone
only this

one

scaled thing

will remain.

RAIN ALWAYS SHUTS DOWN THE PARK

Not every day can be golden, Megga says over the speaker system.
Rides are closed.

No one wants to sit for a portrait in the rain—she sends everyone
who is operating rides home, plus me. Ruth jogs
toward me under a poncho. I let the rain soak me, sad stray dog.

Let's go find Rex.

He's locking up the Loco Loco, and there it is—
crocodile flipping in my gut.

Jesus Christ, I can't even be near the thing, the space
between me and panic like a vertical tube slick with oil.
Nowhere to walk circles, I chant *stop stop stop*
in the circle of my skull, round and round like
one of Wildwood's rides. This place, I think,

is a recipe for disaster. Alarm bells clanging over the sound of Rex's
voice. I have always loved this place, it has always felt like escape,
like rainbow-colored exception, neon-colored candy
for my outstretched hand. But
this is a place where accidents happen, where people like me
are allowed to control the fates of others. This isn't a carnival—
this is a potential crime scene. It's a place of electric impulse and

Ariel, come back

Ruth there on the other side of that nagging voice, her plum frown.

Rex studying the situation, chess player
scriptwriter: *Wanna go to the movies?*

THE DISTANCE BETWEEN ME AND MY BODY

feels like the length of a road trip, cross-country.
I know it's there because it's technically on the map
but reaching out and arriving there seems
like a journey too long to comprehend
with only two legs and no car.

I spend so much time wandering the inside
of my head that I sometimes forget that the head
is on shoulders, that the shoulders attach to a trunk—
arms and legs and feet and ears.

Here I am.

I'm too tall to ignore yet somehow
I am always surprised when I pass a mirror
surprised that as small as I feel in my head
always trying to disappear
I still manage to be here, so largely   here.

I say this to Ruth who says
Because you're major, babe. You're fucking   major.

She laughs out the window when she says it.

I see her smile in the rearview mirror   without
thinking of smashing her teeth.

THERE ARE SO MANY WAYS TO HAVE THE WRONG BODY

Eventually I lose
track.

When I close my eyes and picture
what I would walk inside
if I could choose,
the picture is fractured:

kaleidoscope where some of myself
is thin   small   bending in the breeze
the face at the top
of the neck isn't mine.

Then there is me
but bigger muscles
like their own geography

My body is a planet
that I am too
afraid
to explore.

FINE 5 SHOULD BE FULL

and maybe the other theaters are
but *Legally Blonde* is empty—maybe not Boomer
enough for the typical audience member.

I'm used to being in theaters alone but Rex
is surprised, theorizes that this establishment
is a money-laundering front
while we eat popcorn out of huge buckets.

I ordered my own because what if Ruth
reaches in at the same time and I accidentally
hold her hand? What if she thinks I'm trying to grope her?
Fingers slick with fake butter, trailing up her arm.

> What if you hold her hand? Or what if
> you bite it? You've never been in a theater alone
> with anyone but Leah. And never Fine 5.
> This is your lair, your secret shadowy place
> where you come to hide from your demons. Ruth
> here now like a woman following a wolf into its cave
> Dracula into his castle...

What I like about this movie, says Rex,
is that we never have to see the funeral or even the murder.
All the violence happens off-screen but that doesn't mean
it didn't happen.

Ruth: *Or that the people who are left aren't sad.*

I know you love murder movies, he says, *but yeah.*
We don't need to see it for the message to be delivered.

That's real life, right? Terrible things happening just out of sight
and still mattering more than the things you actually see.

"I DIDN'T GO TO MY COUSIN'S FUNERAL."

Ruth stares at the screen when she says it. We are alone
in the theater, Elle Woods holding a Chihuahua,
hearing confession.

I didn't go to my brother's either, says Rex.

And I could say it out loud—*I didn't go to Felicia Palmer's
funeral*—but then that would beg the question "Who is Felicia
Palmer?" and inevitably someone would ask "How did she die?"

Plus Ruth is still talking:

Everyone at home thinks I don't care. Everyone is so confused
about how my favorite cousin can die and I don't
go to her final resting. Everyone is confused
about how I could walk her to school every day
but not walk down the aisle at church to say goodbye. Everyone
wondering
if we were as close as they thought. Everyone wondering
if I'm cold. Everyone wondering
why she didn't leave a hole in my life
like they think she left in theirs. They think
they understand absence. They think
skipping the funeral is because I didn't want to be there.

How do I explain that it's not that I didn't want
to be there, but that I didn't deserve to be? Absent
when she needed me. Why should I get to say goodbye?

What kind of cousin can't see through
a fake smile?

"IT'S NOT YOUR FAULT."

I say it to the empty theater
I say it to the black ceiling
I say it to Ruth and her long stare
I say it to Rex and his silent tears
and Mandy is too far to hear but I say it to her anyway.

"SOMETIMES I FEEL GUILTY WHEN I DON'T THINK ABOUT HER."

It's been two years but feels like yesterday but time passes and I almost
hate that it hurts less, like I want it to hurt
forever. My family must think it never did.
Sometimes I wonder if my dad sends me to my mom in the summer so
he doesn't have to look at me. Like when he sees my face he sees someone
made of ice.

I know the feeling.
If there was a train to hell, my dad
would buy me a ticket
and strap me in tonight.

Opposite of Ariel, Rex says.
We both look at him.
On-screen, Elle Woods
is giving a speech.

Ariel feels guilty about what she thinks
and you feel guilty about what you don't think
but you both know how you really feel.

Maybe it's cuz I wasn't raised in church
but I don't get how you can feel guilty
about what happens in your head.
I was always told: "As long as you keep it to yourself . . ."

    I ask: *Do you think your brother ever did?*
    Feel guilty about what was happening
    in his head?

I think what was happening in his head
was too loud to think around.

On-screen, the judge bangs the gavel.
I just want to cry.

MEMORY: ABC RUG IN KINDERGARTEN

Crisscross applesauce, my legs already long,
sometimes bumping the girl next to me, Prudence—
Prudence oblivious, open-mouthed listening to Mrs. Grayson,
her colorful posters of feelings.

How do you think Roy is feeling right here?

Roy is a white boy on a vibrant poster,
face like a fire-engine, teeth bared.

Mad, we all chorus.

And what about here?
Fingernail tapping the next poster—
Roy with a dramatic frown
big, blue tears.

Sad!

What about here? See Roy's smile?

Happy!

Yes, or proud! See his painting? He's proud.

We are obedient: *Proud!*

And what about here?

There's Roy, eyes downcast, hands tucked away.

We are silent, eyes prying, trying to
guess.

Ashamed, says Mrs. Grayson. *Roy is ashamed.*

RUTH: "I KNOW WHAT I FEEL"

The problem is, I don't express it in a way that other people can digest.

*My heartbreak is a pit at the heart of the peach, my grief is the skin
of an orange, watermelon rind:*

*it's at the edge, it's at the center, it is seed and flesh and peel.
But for so many people there is only one way to be sad.*

*Why do you think I want to be an actress?
Maybe if I can teach myself to perform the absence of my cousin
my father will look me in the eye again.*

I'M NOT A MOVIE STAR

I'm not on-screen
I don't want anyone
to look at me

so why do I have to follow
a script

my life is not meant
to fit on the stage

and anyway the costume
I choose will need
to be custom-made
because jeans
off the rack will never
     fit

God I'm sick of stage directions
I'm an artist, not an actor

No wonder
I'm so fucking
    tired.

WHEN THE CREDITS ROLL

We sit and watch the current of faceless names in the dark until
the doors behind us crack open, admitting the guy who sometimes
works the concession stand. *Memory: the first time I came to Fine 5,
he and a coworker taking my money for Junior Mints and talking
about how big my hands were as I walked away.* Now, in the dark,
he doesn't notice us until we get up to leave. He knows my face—
I see the spark of recognition. I am the strange regular. Subtle sneer
until he notices Ruth, features smoothing, turning his face into
something human-wolfish.

The bucket to myself, I'd eaten only a fourth of my popcorn. The
rest of it ends up on the floor at his feet. Ruth shout-laughing *OH
MY GOD, ARIEL*

The three of us running out into the daylight. I can hear my own
laughter.

No doubt about the crocodile. This was all me.

STILL RAINING

and we take refuge in Ruth's car, panting. The storm on the roof
is loud and we sit listening. At the entrance of Fine 5, the guy with
the broom emerges, looking around, looking for us.

I'm not even going to ask, Ruth says.

    Nothing to tell. That dude is a dick.

I am ashamed of so many things, but not this. With the rain above
and around us, it's suddenly very clear. My brain is a shame engine.
The train chugging longer and longer, car by car.
    I don't think I can go back there now.

Bummer, says Rex. *I liked that place.*

TRAIN

My brain is sap-sticky. All it takes is a word—
    train—and I'm slingshotted
through the windshield
all the way to Wildwood, where the Loco Loco
rattles on its track, faster and louder
until it crashes through the quiet of this car
into my lap. My hands are always full of blood.

But I can prevent this. I can control this.
I can stop all the bad things the crocodile conjures—
tracing the shape of the windshield
is like a tourniquet around a gunshot.

Is it doing it? Ruth turned around in her seat, peering.
Is your brain trying to trap you? Abort! Abort! Tell it no!

> *I know Mandy says thoughts aren't facts. But*
> *don't they   matter? I wouldn't*
> *just think things for no reason, OCD aside. Would I?*

Ruth looks up through the moonroof at the weeping sky,
considering. *Does everything matter? I don't think so. Like*
TV. Is it important or true or good just because
it's on TV? If it's The Kardashians *or* Tucker Carlson
you can recognize it's garbage and let it pass.

I hear her but I can't hear her. So much
at stake, she and Rex so close, close
enough to break or burn, both
staring at me, wondering and probably
fearing. Rex speaks next:
I think we should call your sister.

MANDY IS IN CLASS BUT TEXTS US A PICTURE OF HER NOTEBOOK

I've always loved her handwriting, so precise
and intentional:

Fearful thoughts ≠ unconscious wishes

Intrusive thoughts ≠ impulses

Thoughts ≠ facts

Anxiety/fear → distorts perception

Then she texts:

Let me tell you a story about your amygdala.

VOICE NOTE FROM MANDY WHILE SHE'S ON BREAK: "ONCE UPON A TIME THERE WAS AN AMYGDALA"

She lived in the brain and it was her job to sound the alarm. It wasn't her job to know whether the danger was real or not—that was up to the cortex. It was just her job to send a danger signal, whether the danger was real or imagined. When the amygdala sounds the alarm, the body she protects reacts.

One day there was a scary thought. *What if I killed someone?* And the amygdala heard the thought and said "SCARY!" And the body reacted: sweat, heartbeat, anxiety. But it was just a thought. Not real danger.

Now, in this case, the job of the cortex is supposed to be: "Nope, not a threat. Let it go." But the cortex *didn't* let it go. It said "Hmm that *does* sound scary. Let's make sure that doesn't actually happen."

The amygdala learns very easily how to be fearful—after all, her job is to save your life. So even a whiff of that thought and she screams again and the cortex says "Good job, you are keeping us safe."

And on and on. The danger is not real—what they think is danger is just thoughts. But in the brain, it feels the same. And sometimes the sweat and the heartbeat and the rush of emotions make the

cortex think *See, I could kill someone! I'm fighting so hard to stop!*
But that danger was never really there—it's all a fear response that
the amygdala fired off.

What I'm trying to say, Ariel, is that it's all happening in your
head. Your amygdala is trying her best. And your cortex needs
some sweet-talking. This would all be so much easier if our parents
believed in therapy. For now, figure out your triggers. I have to take
an exam.

REX: "I'M STILL WONDERING"

how do you not believe in something that obviously exists?
All these names for what happens in people's brains
all of it growing legs over millennia:

hysteria
melancholy
Hippocrates and his four humors

we've always been like this
brains like circuit boards
or a box full of snakes
depending on what century you're born in

all of it changing all the time
all of us changing all the time

and it never getting any easier.

PROMISES

At the end of the block, a team of workers is painting a house.
I've watched it lose its roof and the columns
on its porch. They've carved it into a box of right
angles. It has become part of an army
of exact replicas.

When I stand on my porch and look down
the street at the ways they've all become uniform
I can't help but think of them like people—
all scraping the noses off their faces
eyelashes applied with lumpy glue.

Here on this street, a promise is being kept
but I don't know who offered it
and who agreed.

SOME THINGS ARE BETTER DONE ALONE.

The doubting disease mutates, shifts the goalposts
a win is only a win for the time it takes
for my brain to flip the game board.

With this head, I am always on my toes.

So on Tuesday I check the Wildwood schedule
and on Wednesday arrive an hour before Ruth and Rex
and sit at the darts where Ms. Linda works

> *Can I just sit*

I say

> *Can I just sit and be quiet*

It's a free country, she tells me.
And I know what Leah would say: *Not really.*

But I just say thanks and wait for the kids to come
the ones whose hands I'm always thinking of stabbing
the ones whose palms I imagine blood-slicked

and I dare myself to be brave on my own
dare myself to look the crocodile in the eye
and say

> *You're not even a crocodile.*
> *You're just a little slab of sticky meat,*
> *and it's time to pipe the fuck down.*

A GIRL COMES WITH HER HANDS FULL OF TICKETS

Working here, I've come to know kids like her:
allowance money in her pocket and fire in her heart.

She wants the green dragon, as big as she is
plush as royal carpet. She will not stop
until she gets it, is prepared to use every ticket
at her disposal, every cent of allowance.

She's so small.   **You could break her arm.**

Why? What is wrong with you?

There is nothing wrong with me.
It's just a thought and everyone has them
and I can let it pass

How can you say everyone has them? Normal people aren't
supposed to think like that. Plus you're a girl don't you think
you should be a little less—

Everyone has these thoughts. There is nothing wrong with me.

Sweat and heartbeat. Dizzy on the stool
where I perch like a sick parrot.

The girl throws dart after dart, and I make myself
stay, even while my hands clench around the metal
of the stool.   **You could grab her arm and break it.**

**Would she scream, would her arm bleed
or just wobble, splinters of bone inside,
extracted with tweezers, who did this to you,
what kind of monster...**

There is nothing wrong with me. These
are just thoughts. Thoughts do not equal action.

I imagine my amygdala, sticky, sticky
electric meat, stuck inside the shell
of my skull and shrieking

Alert alert! Scary! Threat!

Cortex always trying to decide.

They are trying to help. God, you
poor babies, you're trying so hard.

Listen to me now—
I'm Ariel, and I'm here
to tell you that my hands
are on this stool, I'm not
going to hurt anyone
because these are just
thoughts and you,
    little brain,
need a vacation.

The balloon pops are never   louder
than the noise in my head

but gradually I'm aware of six in a row

    pop pop pop pop pop pop

and the girl is beaming and Ms. Linda
is passing the green dragon across the counter
and I'm still here

and when the girl looks at me, happy,
alive and happy,
perceived in her moment of glory,
I'm still here

and she's still here
and all I can say is

Hell yeah, kid, you did it

IS THIS HOW IT STARTS?
I always pictured getting off this ride
as a flying leap through shattering
glass, but maybe this
is how it starts:

one inch
one little step
one little handshake
with myself.

WE RIDE THE FERRIS WHEEL ON BREAK
me and Ruth and Rex—
me and Ruth
on one side
Rex on the other.

We let the wind
rock us.

What is everyone thinking about?
Ruth asks the wind
and Rex answers.

I'm thinking about what
would have saved Richard,
he says. *What would have kept*
my brother alive?

Ms. Linda stops us
at the top. She's on the ground
and can't see us
but she knows we're here
and offers this small
act of love.

"MY PARENTS DID THE BARE MINIMUM"

They thought pills were a cure
and not a tool.

I remember the day they found out
that the cop who killed Richard
wouldn't be charged—

I was home and I just kept hearing Mom
scream You promised! You
promised!

My dad did the chief of police's taxes
for fourteen years. White people,
we always think it will be different
for us, and it usually is
*   until it's not.*

We think it will keep us
safe.

I don't know what
would have saved Richard's life.

But I do know my dad doesn't do
the chief's taxes anymore.

HOW CAN A GIRL JUST DIE?

Cloudless blue sky
twenty pairs of legs
twenty hearts
    pushing blood through
    twenty breathing bodies

When one stops
what does it mean?

Does it mean nothing?

I need it to mean
something

or what
is this
all
for?

FELICIA, I NEVER KNEW

your sister's name but I saw her on social media today
Jasmine Palmer, ninth-grade award for science.

I can't help it—I picture her like Mandy:
sifting through the knowledge of the world
to find out what happened to her sister.

Good sister, tracking down the truth,
asking all the questions that keep her up at night:
How did this happen? How did this happen?

Groping through the dark for a cause.

I stared at her photo, purple braces.
I almost left a comment:
It was me. I'm right here.

CROCODILE LAWYERS

*Do you or do you not agree that you were present the day of Felicia
Palmer's death?*

*Do you deny that you were staring at her in the moment that her heart
stopped?*

*Do you deny the possibility—nay, the probability—that you caused
this promising young woman's death with the intensity of your evil
stare?*

Do you deny that your proximity was such that whatever curse enshrines you was close enough to produce this tragic event?

My arguments are always weak. What do you say? The lawyers are always so sure. Somehow it feels like they're on my side. They want to make sure everyone is safe. They want to make sure this never happens   again.

IF THIS IS GOING TO WORK

then I have to be vigilant.
Mandy's words have become a tattoo:

> **Thoughts are not impulses**
> **Thoughts are just thoughts**

Ruth has taken to blurting out her own:

Just pictured that guy naked

Just thought about going to the store and buying eggs to throw on that car

Just thought about a huge alien foot coming down from the sky and crushing us

Just wondered if that lady has a bomb in her purse

Just thought about my cousin and wondered if she cried when she did it

We are suits of flesh. We are electric
meat. We fire and misfire.

We just want to be happy.

"HAPPY IS JUST AN ELECTRIC OCCURRENCE,"

Rex tells us. He says that happiness is a chemical.
That if someone can't feel happy
it's not because they're not trying
but because maybe their brain just doesn't
make enough of the thing we
physiologically need to experience
the emotion we know as "happy."

That's where medication can be useful.

He has a certain voice he uses when he talks about his brother—
I imagine Richard as sweet and wild, a beehive of a boy.

I don't think I want medication, I say. *I can*
figure this out. I can fix this myself.

Maybe so, he says.
But would you say that about a broken arm?

RUTH WANTS TO RIDE THE TILT-A-WHIRL

by herself. *Sit there,* she orders us:
Perceive me!

We perceive her.
She spins round and round
sometimes laughing
sometimes staring at us straight-faced
as the ride rolls her, metallic ocean.

When did you know, I ask.

When I was a toddler, he says. *Girlhood like a squeaky wheel, never oiled by tomboy or blue shirts. Boyhood like an oasis in a desert. Boyhood the only thing that felt like water. It felt like love. As soon as I saw it. Does girlhood feel like an itchy sweater? Like shoes too small?*

It's not that. I don't want to be a boy. I just want
to be the kind of girl
I am. I   think.

Then you should be.

Maybe so. And when did you know?

When did I know what?

Ruth laughing like a kookaburra. My heart,
oh god, inside a fist.

That you loved her.

Right away, he says. *Right away.*

THIS WORLD

already too small
for me, and me
feeling myself
growing
still

still
growing

god if I was smaller
I would hide me
from myself

if only
to make these
feelings
smaller
too.

IN FIRST GRADE A BOY PULLED MY HAIR

so hard a chunk came out. I punched
his loose tooth onto the desk.

When I was 13 I asked Mandy if she remembered.

She said *More than menstruation, it's these things
that define us as women. If a boy is pulling your hair
that's how you know
you're a girl.*

I just can't agree.

I want more from this life and this body
than choosing its place
based on pain.

I saw someone on social media say they knew
they were cis because gender was never
a squeaky wheel in the bicycle of their identity—

but I don't know about that either:
my girl-wheel is always squeaking

but I don't know if it's because it actually needs
oil or because everyone is always putting a stick
in my spoke.

ALL I WANT IS TO CHOOSE.

I want to choose what to pick up
and what to throw away

I want to wear what fits
I want to donate the rest

I want the thoughts I want
and I want the rest
to fall away

I want to be a sheep in the mountains:
someone shear me of all this extra mess.

Maybe I'll stay naked
maybe I'll grow it back
maybe I'll use it all to make
a sweater
that doesn't itch

The point is
I want to choose

Is that so hard?
Jesus Christ I just want
to   choose.

EXPOSE YOURSELF

The thing about riding the bus
is that if the goal is to be exposed
to what you're afraid of,
you will be.

Not just the thoughts
in your own head

but the kind of men who hold
on to the bar over your seat,
crotch at eye level

everyone around you too polite
to ask him what the fuck
he's doing.

Maybe I have to be
the one, and maybe

this is magic too—
the belief that by delivering
the right   *fuck you*
at the right time
I can plant the seed
that keeps this crotch
out of other girls' faces.

If anything, this
is what defines my   womanhood:
not what he does to me
but what I do for us

nameless faceless siblings
even the ones whose parents
gave them a different name
at first.

I don't know what I feel
about the span of my
shoulders, but I know
how I feel about   you
how I would place you there
on my back

and carry you
if I could.

TEXTS WITH RUTH AND REX

Ruth: First kiss, go

Rex: Shula Berea in 5th grade. She smelled like spearmint. We were wearing roller skates

Ariel: I don't count the first time. Brent and his fat wet tongue.
I count Crystal Greenidge, school bus on a field trip

Rex: Ruth . . . ?

Ruth: I've never kissed anyone

Ariel: what

Rex: wait . . . EVER?!

Ruth: It just never happened. I think I'm overthinking it

Ariel: I get that

INVISIBLE CASTLE

The more I think about what I'm supposed to be

1. Girl.
2. Sister.
3. Daughter.
4. Friend.

The less I care about
1–3
and the more I focus
on 4

There's so many rules
to gender
and I don't think it's even
that I'm nonbinary

it's just that my eyes
have adjusted to see
the invisible castle
where all these boxes
are supposed to be stored

and it turns out
they're invisible too.

We're all just holding the box
someone shoved into our hands
all the props and wardrobes
packed in tightly.

And every day that I'm breathing
my skin replacing itself every moment

the more I realize I like to
pack light.

STANDING IN THE HALL LISTENING

to my father wash his hands.

He's awake before my mother,
awake before the sun.

When I enter the kitchen
he turns off the water
stands in the silence I bring
with me.

How many times a day do you wash your hands?

What are you doing awake?

Couldn't sleep

Just finishing up here.

How many times a day do you wash your hands?

He looks so tired.

Why are you asking me that?

I'm just curious.

Cleanliness is next to godliness.

How many?

As many as it takes.

IF YOU'RE LISTENING, GOD,

it's not that I don't believe
in you   or even that I do

it's just that things
have gotten complicated
in this last year: every time
I go to pray, the words
turn urgent orange   transform
into something sticky.

Can you believe in god
and magic at the same time?

I think I have magicked
myself into a corner, lord,
and I know my father
still believes in you
but I think he has too:

he never says much
out loud but I'm beginning
to recognize the space
around him
as something familiar—

I think his silences are filled
with something sticky
and I know that the stickiness
doesn't leave much room
for the kind of prayer that feels   good

so

if you can, god,
pay him a visit.

Fill up those empty places
with your love. I'm realizing
that he needs some help

I'm realizing that he's up against
something that no one but you
can see.

HURT PEOPLE

hurt people.

My father
is hurting me

and there is no
"but"

only "and":

my father
is hurting me

and he is
hurting
too.

OUR FATHERS CAN'T LOOK IN OUR EYES

Something between us and them
too thick to get around

grief like a wall and ivy,
loss and more loss.

I want my father to look me in the eye
and say what he's afraid of.
I want to know if there's a voice
telling him I'm unclean
or if in his mind   like mine
the dirty thing is him:

if he's always out the window
so he won't put me through the glass.

I want Ruth's father to look her in the eye
and instead of looking for tears,
look for pain—
the quiet kind.

We're not always screaming,
we're not always fainting onto couches—
sometimes pain is a siren
sometimes it is an envelope closing in on itself
sealing itself into the future
traveling miles before it opens.

I want Rex's father to look him in the eye
and see that he may have lost one son
but he still has one left.

ONE STEP FORWARD

two steps back.

Today getting on the bus to Wildwood
feels impossible—
the frothing swamp too green.

I walk.

Will it always be
like this:
some days shallow
and some days deep
some days able to walk on water
some days full of sinking

How do you evict a reptile?
It can't read.

Ariel, it's not a reptile at all—
it's your own pink sticky brain
just doing the best it can
to keep you alive
and everyone else
safe.

"CAN YOU DRAW ME REAL?"

the girl wants to know.
She's my age with a shaved head,
the remaining fuzz dyed pink.

With no one in line, I take my time
on her. I bring her to life. I use
too much ink and I don't mind
when it smears down my arm

I feel good and dirty.
I wonder if I have ink on my face—
I hope I do.

You have an artist's hands,
the girl says. *Like you play the piano.*
Do you?

    No, just this.

I think I can see myself like she sees me
if I look hard and don't blink.

On the paper, her magenta head
is like a rising sun.
She tells me she's Filipina, asks if I like
jazz. She has so many questions
and with the pens in my hands
I answer and answer and answer.

When I'm finished, her face stares up at me
impish, round-cheeked.

She says, *Can you write my name on there too?*
And when I do she says
Now my number.

I do.

She smiles.
There, she says, *now you keep it.*

I RIDE A GIRAFFE

in long slow circles.

Beside me, Ruth is flying
a Canadian goose.

Rex sits sidesaddle
on a cheetah.

What is a girl
What is a boy
What is adulthood
What is growing up

We're just going around in circles
and the music doesn't match
how we all feel

We're all feeling a million
different things.

I miss my brother, Rex says
I miss what we missed
I hate the bridges that a death builds
September 7th
Dairy Queen—

those things cannot exist
separately from the bullets
in his back,
the one in his chin.

The giraffe lifts me toward the ceiling
then pulls me back down.

Endless.

Then people say "see, cops don't kill just *Black people"*
like this makes it better

Like this absolves the cops instead of indicting them.

Who wins when you say that? he asks the goose.
Nobody wins. Everybody's dead.

IT'S MIDNIGHT AND I COULD BE SLEEPING

but instead I'm making grilled cheese.
It's the only thing I know how
to make.

Memory:
Mandy when her hair was still long
showing me how to layer the cheese, Miracle
Whip in a thin layer on the outside of the bread.

Stove on low-medium so it doesn't smoke.

This oven is fancier than where she taught me
but the knobs are the same—I know
how to make the fire burst high then turn it low.

Click of gas.

This is an old ritual—
I haven't cooked in a year
and when I learned, it wasn't so I could feed a child,
I didn't learn to audition for marriage.

Ritual passed from sister to sister:

This is how you feed yourself
This is how you make it taste good
This is how you create something
     that keeps your body not just alive
          but happy.

WHEN MY MOTHER SITS AT THE COUNTER

I think it's morning
because once in her room for the evening
she doesn't usually come out.

I barely recognize her
    face pale
in this light and without makeup
she looks older
wrinkles around her eyes
frown line between her brows.

Smells good, she says

    Want one?

It takes her a long time
to say *okay.*

When we eat, we do it
silently.

> Butter knife isn't sharp enough to cut
> without huge force. You're strong enough
> to do it. How long would it take to
> saw off her—

These are just thoughts.
These are the Tucker Carlson
of thoughts and I can let them
        go.

Through the kitchen window,
the lights in the house next door
are still on. Not the lights of a home
but bald bulb and string.

Under construction.

I KNOW I'M NOT MEANT TO BE AN ACTOR—

the script is one way and life
is another

my brain a spinning globe.

My body likes to change
its mind and what is a body

but a ticking clock
one twitch away from explosion
or epiphany?

How does what's between my legs
have a gender
but my eyeballs do not

Don't they do something different
when trained

·Can't my hands be taught
to be   to do
what my mind imagines

My mind has been imagining
blood for so long

blood and behemoth—

once I reroute the highway
in my head

who knows what I'll do
and where I'll look,

who knows what and who
I'll touch?

These hands   when my amygdala
and my cortex have made a gentle
truce   will go on being hands
and these eyes

will go on looking,
though what they see
will be different.

IT'S 2AM AND I'M ON REX'S FRONT PORCH

On the way through the dark,
stepping over sidewalk chalk
that little kids forgot
ghosts they left behind
on the pavement.

Got your text, Rex says. You
brought me something?

   Grilled cheese.

Sweet.

He eats.

   I'm sorry about your brother.

Me too.

His chairs don't rock
or sway
but we   do.

RUTH SHOWS UP AT SUNRISE WITH DONUTS.

You could have texted me sooner.

   We didn't want to wake you up.

I was awake.

We talk in whispers
and leave crumbs.

   *What are you most
   afraid of?*

Missing the signs, she says.
Again and again. Losing everyone.
Getting to the edge
a second   too late.

Him: *Never leaving this town.*
Getting stuck in invisibility.

Answer your own question, Ariel.

> *Hurting the people*
> *I love and not being able*
> *to stop.*

THERE ARE STILL THINGS I DON'T SAY

Thoughts and thoughts
some of them bloody
and some of them wet
with pink-tongued saliva.

But what I don't say
on this porch
surrounded by crumbs

is

I am afraid no one
will ever love me.

I am afraid
I will never be ready.

Maybe one day
love like a hole in the curtain:

light pouring through
warm and wanted.

Maybe before I reach
before I let it in

this curtain must slide slowly,
eyes adjusting—

let my pupils settle
before it all rushes in.

"I THINK WE SHOULD TRY AGAIN"
I hear him but don't answer.

I think it's time to try
the train.

Oh baby amygdala
I hear you shouting

you're so used to taking care
of everyone else

you don't know how
to be taken care of

but I'm working
on it   I swear.

EVENTUALLY I LEAVE THEM ON THE PORCH
and at first I walk without looking back,
afraid that looking
will show them
sitting closer together
than when I left.

But when I step past the curb
I glance back and see her head
on his shoulder
his hand
on her knee

and I feel the warmth
of both their bodies
as if pressed
against
my own heart.

LIKE A KNIFE

Fearful thoughts ≠ unconscious wishes

Intrusive thoughts ≠ impulses
Thoughts ≠ facts

I have to be careful
with words like these.

Spoken too closely
together
and with magic
in mind

they become
mantra

they become
ritual.

What do you need to unglue
a brain this
sticky?

ON THE WAY HOME I FIND THE CHALK AGAIN

I spend a long time in front of each house
on my block, moonlight white
and me unwatched.

I write until the chalk is dust, the same words up and down
the block. When the neighborhood watch wakes up
my mother and her Lycra friends
        the ones with the cops on speed dial
they will read it and only one
of them won't wonder who:

WHY DO YOU WANT TO LIVE HERE?

IS HOME MORE LIKE HOME WHEN
IT'S   CONQUERED

IS HOME MORE LIKE HOME
WHEN IT'S   ALL THE SAME

HAVE YOU EVER
ASKED YOURSELF   WHY?

TEXTS WITH MANDY IN THE MORNING

Ariel: so what am I supposed to do instead of counting

Ariel: I just refuse? Do something else?

Ariel: Google says when I have a violent thought to turn it into a joke

Ariel: you're in class aren't you. I'm sorry

Mandy: sorry

Ariel: it's okay, I will figure this out

I HAVE FOUR HOURS UNTIL I NEED TO BE AT WORK

Inside my house the sound
of jackhammer construction racket
pounds through the window.

I stand at the counter, knife drawer within
reach. For the first time in a long time
I'm not afraid of what I will do.

I am afraid of what I won't do. I am afraid
I will never leave this house. I am afraid
I will stop noticing the jackhammer.

I'm afraid I will sink into this swamp
and walk through Target with my lip curled
at hair growing where hair grows.

I told Rex and Ruth I am afraid
of hurting the people I love but also
I am afraid of the people I love hurting
me, and me not loving myself
enough to stop them.

IT'S FRIDAY AND I HAVE SOMEWHERE TO BE.

Sky like ashes
but no rain.

It doesn't
matter.

As long
as the door
is unlocked.

IT IS.

Inside, the fans whir slow
and lazy

the room is full
of breath
and metal

Mr. Cipinko
shelving weights.

He is the same.

It is all
the same.

When he sees me,
his eyes twinkle.

Ready to get back on?

I DIDN'T BRING CLOTHES

I sweat right through my purple polo
and every drop feels
human.

"YOU'RE GOING TO HAVE TO START SLOW"

You can't expect more than you're able to give—
strength is patience
and patience is strength.

He has his own orbit—
his own burdens
to lift—

and I lift
mine.

When he notices
me struggling
he calls

Grit it out.
Your mind
and your body
are in this
together.

WHAT A STRANGE ACTIVITY,

lifting weights. Grip heavy object, hold it
tight. Then lift it. Then let it
down. Then lift it again. And again
until your body speaks in a tremble.

These are the times it's easy
not to think of blood. I don't think
of anything. I am all marvel
and no prayer.

Not too big or too
hard, but merely
in motion.

SOON MEGGA'S TRAILER WILL BE FILLED WITH BOXES

but not yet. Soon she'll be packing up the summer
before she migrates to her next adventure. For now,
she's in there with her feet on her desk, corn dog in her hand.

Megga, do you have an extra shirt I can wear today?

I don't tell her mine stinks of sweat.

I'd forgotten the specific
kind of tired that comes with lifting.

My body screams and sings.

Megga tosses a shirt across her desk, then brandishes
the corn dog.

Might make them vegan next year, she says.
I know a girl. We'll see. Give it a try.

She passes the food across the desk
and I would ordinarily never eat after someone
not family, but my mother would shrink me to fit
in her fist if she could, so what is family
really, if not a country you can be cast
out of, before finding somewhere else
to make a home?

I take a bite. *It tastes fine,* I say.

Just fine?

    No, good. It tastes good.

Are you still having a hard time?

    Yes. But maybe a little softer.

I TELL HER MORE ABOUT OCD,
what I'm beginning to understand.

And your parents don't believe in therapy?

    Prayer cures all.

Do you believe that?

    No.

What do you believe?

    That my brain has a problem. And problems have solutions. I don't need therapy if I know the problem on my own.

I pass the corn dog back and she thinks
while she chews.

I wasn't informed, she says.

    About what?

About you dropping out of high school.

    Huh? I didn't.

I hadn't heard that you left school early and got a degree in psychology.

    Megga, what?

She swallows the last bite. There's mustard on her lip
and her cat eyes glow.

I'm glad you will survive. Baby you have been struggling so hard. But I will tell you what your mother won't: you need a doctor. And maybe you can't do that right now. But as soon as you can, you go. Find a

clinic. Something. Don't think that you alone can soothe a burn that
an emergency room would treat. If your neck were broken, would you
wrap it in a towel? Duct tape? I've got this? No.

It's not the same, Megga.

Oh but it is. Your brain has to live in that body. It needs care. The real
kind.

"YOU LOOK LIKE YOU JUST GOT OUT OF THE POOL," SHE SAYS THEN.

So sweaty.

I just laugh.

The shirt she gave me is 3XL
and hangs off me like a tent.

I hear my mother's voice: *wear something*
that fits. People will think you're a boy

But the bagginess feels good. I feel   good.

Are you going to college next year?

From anyone else this question would feel
too heavy, even for me. I would be searching
the script for the right line. Here in her trailer, I can sigh.

Honestly, Ms. Megga, I have no idea. About anything.

She stands from her desk, and when she opens her arms
for a hug the thought crosses my mind that I
will squeeze too tight. That there's

**a reason I haven't hugged anyone in 10 months.
There's a reason I don't touch anyone, that I
can't be touched.
What if I hug her and then
can't stop and my hands end up
around her
neck...**

But I hug her, and I tell myself that these
are just thoughts. I am allowed
to have them and then let them go.

If you have no idea about anything, she says, *then I think you're on the
right track. If you thought you had it all figured out, that's when I'd
be worried. Look at it this way: now you have less to unlearn.*

But what if everything goes bad, I whisper.

What if what if what if...

Then it goes bad. She shrugs
when she lets me go. *But you can always come back here.*

"SHE'S NOT WRONG"

texts Mandy when I tell her what was said.

Mandy: This isn't a permanent solution, you know that, right? This is for now. Band-Aid, not stitches.

Ariel: You think my brain needs stitches?

Mandy: Whose doesn't? Who isn't walking around in the world needing to be put back together?

CARNIVAL GIRL

I've always thought
that this was the place for me.

Wild and weird.
Unpredictable.
Left of center.

On this one thing
I might have been right

SO MUCH OF LIFE IS ABOUT THREAT

Ape-ancestors,
fight or flight
wired into the meat.

But threat is not just
rustling bushes, shadow
and hiss.

Threat is a string of diamonds
brandished at my neck.

Threat is the conjurings
of my own pink brain.

And then there is me
weapon-bodied

accidentally aimed
at the rule book
that the world
thumps
like a Bible.

The ground feels
solid under my feet.

I am so massive
that if I lean too far
I might tip
this whole boat,
all the rules
splashing into the
sea.

What then?

When boxes
of boy
and girl

and man
and woman

sink down
to swim with
the sharks?

What happens
when they dissolve?

When everyone sees
they couldn't
hold water
to begin with?

I DRAW PORTRAITS

and try not to think about the Loco Loco—
from where I sit I can see it
can hear the kids screaming.

When I worked the ride I could always tell
the difference between the scared screams
and the happy ones.

Sometimes I would stop the ride
early if a kid was too freaked out:

I know how it feels
to be on a ride and think you'll never get off

that no one is watching or listening
to notice you need to escape.

I wonder if any of the serial killers
whose childhoods I know by heart
ever chose mercy.
Are there some things a brain
is just not built for?
Memory: babysitter.
Solve all their tiny massive problems.

Maybe this is what I am
no matter where I am.

THE GIRL WITH THE PINK HAIR IS BACK

trying to pay for another portrait
    You don't need to pay, I say.

You didn't call me, she answers.

She sits in the chair and I sketch her—
black pen instead of the colors of caricature.

Do you have a girlfriend or something?

Down the lane of Wildwood I hear Ruth
laughing. I would know her laugh in a sea
of laughs. I could reach in my hand and pull it out.

Do I want Ruth to be my girlfriend?
Or do I want her to be my person?

I feel her love for me when she drives
us in the booming silence of the wind

"Get in, loser."

She sees me and I see her.
Do I want to kiss her
or is what I actually want
to know her forever
and forever?

No, I don't, I tell the girl, surprised by my own smile.

Then what? You're not interested?

I draw her eyebrows. They are dark
and soft compared to the brilliant pink
nothing of her hair.

How did you know I'm into girls?

She laughs. Oh what a laugh. Music and mystery.

I can just tell. I speak your language.

I draw her chin, her ears.

Why are you blushing?

   I'm not.

Yes you are. Why?

   You're beautiful.

Her smile is noon. *I know.*

HER NAME IS ELISA.

This time
she puts her number in my phone.
Her hands are small and move
quickly across my cracked screen.

What happened to your phone? she asks.

   I threw it at a guy who was bothering my friend

Knight in shining armor. She grins.

She sends herself a text from my phone.

I don't mind.

WHEN RUTH EATS A FUNNEL CAKE

she destroys it.

*You're supposed to pull it apart piece
by piece,* Rex yells. *What are you doing?*

She picks up the whole thing, eats it
like a sandwich.

You're a monster, he gasps.

I am Ruth, conqueror of worlds

When she talks, she sprays powdered
sugar in white clouds.

Such a lady, he says

You're goddamn right

I LOVE THEM

Oh god, I love them

If I run now
then maybe
they'll remain
unharmed.

Are we going to do this? Rex asks me.

You can do it, Ruth says.

    That's what I'm afraid of.

MEMORY: ME AND LEAH

walking to the park. Felicia has been dead
for four months
and when I ask Leah if she has thought
about her
she says *Who?*

I should have known then
that some people can be hurt
but then let it go

I can't let anything
go.

REX HAS A PLAN

to expose me, luring
out the crocodile
with double bait.

The train itself
but Rex and Ruth onboard—

the kiddie park closed down
and the rock music
from the rest of Wildwood
not quite reaching.

We trust you, he says

   But why

We know you

   Are you sure

*Ariel, what better way
to prove to yourself?*

*You're afraid you'll hurt someone you love
This is how you show yourself that you're okay*

   But what if I'm not

But what if you are?

RUTH IS QUIET.

Since that day on the bridge
Ruth screaming
*Were you going to do it?
Were you going to jump?*

I have caught her looking empty:
tree of birds without songs.

Even when she's laughing I see something familiar—
void within a void.

Somewhere inside I'm afraid
that she wants to get on this train
because she believes
the scales inside me
will make all the roaring sadness
quiet.

I want to prove her wrong.
But more than that I want
her birds to sing
again.

I want her so full she's
overflowing.

AN HOUR UNTIL CLOSING

I text Leah. This time

I say more:

I just want you to know
that I understand

I know I didn't
make it easy. I don't blame you
for outgrowing me when my clouds
filled all the space.

She's taken shelter in DC from Hurricane Ariel
      tempest in silent disguise.

I wonder what she'll think
when she sees me again, if
she'll notice I have torn
pieces of myself out

If she'll think I'm getting worse
when somehow I know
it means I'm getting better.

I didn't expect an answer this fast
but I haven't even put my phone down
when she replies:

You can't outgrow
what you're made for.

RUTH DANGLES THE KEYS TO THE LOCO LOCO

When Rex is in her sight
her crooked parts are laid straight.

He lifts her without touching

There is something in him that makes her
grow.

We are all made
for more than
one thing.

There are so many things
that are made for us.

ACROSS THE PARK, THE MUSIC

begins. I am all snake
and swamp
and
shiver.

I don't want to hurt the people I love
not Leah
not my father

Not Rex and Ruth.
And I love them,
this
girl and boy
all the choices
they've chosen

climbing into the last seat of the Loco Loco
his hand extended to help her across the gap.

I love them, his hand on the small of her back
I love them, her braids swinging while she finds the seat belts
I love them, their jokes that fly like sparks off fire

Their trust in me
their trust in their own young guts.

They believe there's something in me that doesn't slither.
Something in me that walks upright with round pupils.

They want me to be amazed
They want to be unfazed

We are electric meat
firing and misfiring
We just want to be happy
with each other.

THE KEYS JINGLE CLEAR AND SILVER

Memory: my first summer at Wildwood
Mr. Malcolm training me and Leah on every machine
especially this one.

This one seems the simplest, he says.
Because it's slow.

Don't let it get too hot—
we don't want any derailings
of the slowest train in the country.

Would the worry have ever planted
its flag if he never said it?
When I put the keys
into the silver dash, I realize

the crocodile is a phantom—
overactive amygdala
inventing a shadow.

These are thoughts
and I'm allowed to have them
There is space in this brain for doubt
and worry
but there is also space in this brain for hope

There is room enough for love and lust.
There is room enough for me.

WHEN I TURN THE KEY

Everything hums. The lights
turn on, Loco Loco and its sparkle
of green and blue and white.

Memory: eating nachos in the caboose
while Leah rode ahead,
Brian's arm around her shoulders.

Slow and slow
the sky so blue it could melt
into a puddle.

Me keeping my eyes away
from my best friend

What if people think I'm jealous
     what if I am
What if Leah thinks I want her for myself
What if I do
Clingy girl
Strange lesbian
Leah deserves better than this.

(But she's my best friend.
Made for each other.)

Out of your head! Ruth screams.

She's buckled in.

*Come back down to Mars
with the rest of us
weirdos!*

THE TRAIN BEGINS TO MOVE

under my hand

Who would ever
trust me this much

My fingers want to press all the buttons
My hand wants to wrap up the lever
and push it toward   oblivion.

Screaming gears
Screaming throats

This could be the last day
for us all.

Or this could be the first day
of the rest of
my life.

THE TRAIN CLIMBS THE FIRST HILL

Then down
This is the first place the children scream

Ruth and Rex shriek

They are laughing

The cars are so small
because they're for children

but what's the space between children
and us?

I have my feet in so many camps—
I haven't decided which one is safest
and I know we can't always choose.

His arm is around her shoulders in the smallness of the car.

She leans into him—for her, he is shelter.

Hurricane Ariel.

But then I remember
that in *The Tempest,*
the little devil made the storm
but he also   made it rest.

ARIEL CRASHES A TRAIN

Ariel Slits a Throat
Ariel Drives Knife Through Beloved Chest
Ariel Chooses the Razor
Ariel Burns Down the House
Ariel Ends a Life

and still

Ariel Wants More
Ariel Loves a Girl
Ariel May Not Be One
Ariel Kills a Crocodile
Ariel Isn't Perfect
Ariel Never Will Be

SOMEWHERE IN WILDWOOD A CHILD HAS WON A YELLOW LLAMA

She used all her money knocking down piles of balls—
she lost enough times for her parents to call it rigged.

But she trusts the luck of her arm.
When it all falls down, she accepts
everything she magicked into existence.

Rex tips his head back against the train seat.
Up then down, hill after tiny hill—
sometimes they whisper;
sometimes they shout to me,
Ruth sharing her passing thoughts,
the ones that make me feel human:

I just thought about a bomb disguised as a shooting star
I just wondered if hedgehogs would eat a finger
I just thought about barfing in Rex's lap, if he would still kiss me after

Absolutely not, he tells her

But he leans in
and from where I stand—
here, the place where the person tasked with caution
remains
the person you trust with your life—

I watch Ruth tilt her face
wind stirring her hair.

When they kiss, the fireworks haven't started yet.

Across the park a woman empties her purse looking for coins—
one more ticket to win her girlfriend that purple unicorn.

I watch   flesh and flesh and flesh.

I watch and I smile and the train rolls on
and I haven't counted anything except the three stars in the sky.

Two people I love kiss each other and I laugh and

everyone is safe.

NOTE FOR READERS

To anyone looking for resources about obsessive-compulsive disorder, here are some places to start:

INTERNATIONAL OCD FOUNDATION

iocdf.org/about-ocd/#obsessions

iocdf.org/faith-ocd

ANXIETY AND DEPRESSION ASSOCIATION OF AMERICA

adaa.org/learn-from-us/from-the-experts/blog-posts/
consumer/demystifying-mental-compulsions-and-pure-o

ACKNOWLEDGMENTS

The year 2020 was a tough one for people with OCD. I mean, let's be clear, it was a tough year for everybody. But some folks with OCD have lived years of their lives being talked out of the belief that there was an ever-looming threat of contamination, and in 2020, it was like being proven right. On Christmas of 2020, my years of undiagnosed OCD came to a head.

I ended up in the ER convinced I was having a heart attack: arm and face numb, unable to breathe, nauseated, sweating. After all the tests and one patiently impatient doctor telling me firmly that I was definitely not having a heart attack and was in fact fine, it was the physician's assistant who said softly when we were alone, "Can I tell you something? I've seen people like you in here. Especially this year. You think you're sick, but you're really just scared. Do you have a therapist? Ask them about OCD."

I didn't have a therapist. It took me two months to crawl out of the hole I was in and find one. And suddenly my life made sense. So in these acknowledgments, I must first say "thank you" to that PA. I'm not sure what would have happened with me had she not said what she said.

Young women spend a lot of time thinking that something is wrong with their bodies—mostly because society spends a lot of time (and money) telling young women that something *is.* The head that OCD rears can wear many different faces, and so many of them strike young women in a specifically painful way.

Sexual intrusive thoughts? *Good girls don't think about sex!*

Violent intrusive thoughts? *Good girls aren't violent!*

Thoughts of contamination? *Girls are supposed to be clean!*

Religious intrusive thoughts? *Good girls are supposed to be without sin!*

Intrusive thoughts about hurting children? *Good girls are supposed to be maternal!*

Extreme concern with things being perfect? *Well, girls* are *supposed to be perfect!*

Fear of "catching" negative character traits? *Birds of a feather! Don't be like those bad girls!*

Thank you to my editor, Liesa Abrams, for immediately understanding the importance of this story—for seeing right to the heart of it: *Why do we think there is something wrong with us?* Thank you to my agent, Patrice Caldwell, and her assistant, Trinica Sampson, for riding along so doggedly during the revision of this book. This was a hard one, wasn't it? I'm so grateful to this team—including the amazing Emily Harburg, as always!—for allowing me the time and space to realize how connected it all is. That our ideas of gender "rightness" are as erroneous as the search for "rightness" in our brains and lives. My deep thanks to Sherronda J. Brown for digging through the mess of everything I was trying to say and pulling out the diamond of truth.

Thank you to my Soulie, Hope Lockett, for walking with

me on this journey. Being able to talk freely about OCD is a big part of undermining its power, and you let me talk endlessly. I love you dearly. Finally, thank you, Omaun Covington, for being so patient for so long, even before I figured out what this was. It can't have been easy, and you never lost patience. I'm forever grateful.

"Dear Reader: Get ready to have your heart beautifully broken."

—BRITTANY CAVALLARO, *New York Times* bestselling author of *A Study in Charlotte*

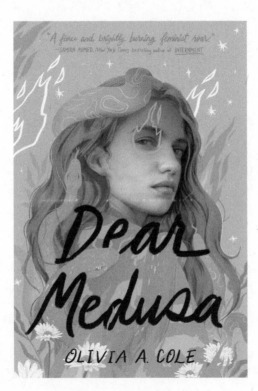

Read on for a glimpse at *Dear Medusa,* the story of Alicia, who's been cast—like the mythical Medusa—as not the victim but the monster of her own story: the "slut who asked for it."

My mother offers to iron my school uniform and even though I want her to, I say no,

because sometimes
    in this place
    where I am

it feels good to refuse
help, because saying yes
to even something like an iron

feels like saying yes
    to everything else

when my whole life
has become a pipe bomb
full of pieces
that explode in a furious
    no.

TUESDAY, SEPTEMBER 4
The school bus stops on my block but I don't get on.

I've been taking the city bus all summer
and I like the way it makes me feel
like I'm living in a different world
than the people who are supposed to be
my peers. What's the difference?

At least on the city bus
I can pull the string,
and it makes me feel
like I'm in control.

I can get off whenever I want
wherever I want
even if my destination
is predetermined.

On the city bus I can still wonder
what the people there think about me,
whereas at school
once I walk through the door
I already know what they're all thinking,
what they're all going
to say
about all the versions of me they think they know,
laid alongside
all the girls I was before
in stark contrast.

Flashbacks

They are like ripples on a pond and they begin
in my earliest memories of myself:

Playing in the fountains at Elwain Park
with no shirt on, five-year-old bird
chest

Eight and pointing at bras in Target, my brother
wearing them like hats while my mother
shopped and I laughed

Sarah getting her first bikini, me ten
and silent and feeling a brand-new envy
grow in like ivy

Me eleven
Me twelve
Me thirteen
Me fourteen

Curious and curious
Me warming up
Me sneaking to buy my first thong
Me excited for someone
        anyone
to notice

Me kissing Michael Strong
the day I got my braces off
just to feel what someone's tongue felt like
sliding across new teeth

Me hearing about what good girls
do and think and say
and always feeling like a neon opposite
even if only in shadow.

Me thinking I had secrets until last year
when I learned what it meant—
        what it really meant—
to hide.

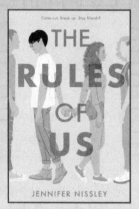

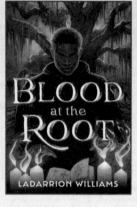